GATEKEEPER'S
CHALLENGE

Eva Pohler

Published by Green Press

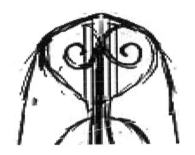

This book is a work of fiction. The characters, happenings, and dialogue came from the author's imagination and are not real.

THE GATEKEEPER'S CHALLENGE. Copyright 2012 by Eva Pohler.

FIRST EDITION

Book Cover Design by Melinda VanLone

Library of Congress Cataloging-in-Publication has been applied for

ISBN -13: 978-0615719283
ISBN-10: 0615719287

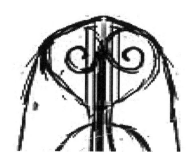

Acknowledgements

I would like to thank my grandparents, Ro Ann and Luther Ouellette and Joe and Margaret Mokry; my parents, Cathy and Joe Mokry; my in-laws and second parents, Danny and Lois Pohler; my siblings, Lisa Hubacek, Rachel Mokry, and Jody Mokry; my husband, David Pohler; and my three children, Mason, Travis, and Candace Pohler. Without them, this book would not have happened. I would also like to thank my book cover designer, Melinda VanLone. Finally, I would like to thank my aunts, uncles, nieces, nephews, critique group, and book club for their help and support.

Chapter One: Sleep and Death

Therese Mills let out a shrill, gleeful scream. "You're back!" She practically flew into Than's arms, running across the gravelly drive of her Colorado log cabin, the small pebbles working their way between her bare feet and flip-flops. She kept saying, "You're back!" over and over with profound disbelief. The ten months since she had last seen him at Mount Olympus over the dead body of Steve McAdams had seemed an eternity.

"You feel so good," Than murmured as his lips caressed her now-moist skin, hot beneath the summer sun and his even hotter body against her. He stopped, ran his fingers through her short, red curls. "Nice."

"Not too short?"

"I love it. Makes your adorable dimples stand out more." He kissed her again, his hands moving along her bare waist. "On your way for a swim?"

She was wearing the same bikini from last summer, the one she wore shortly after she and Than had met at Jen's ranch down the road. She smiled now at the memory of their swim in the lake. The lake was actually a reservoir tucked in a small valley between the San Juan Mountains. Only five homes, including hers and Jen's, spread apart and wedged in the mountains, shared this spectacular view.

"Care to join me?"

"What about your aunt and uncle?"

"They're inside, working. They won't bother us."

He covered her with more kisses.

They were kissing on her gravelly drive one minute and at the bank the next, holding hands on the jetties, about to jump. A hawk soared over the valley beneath the early morning sun.

"Did we just god travel?" Therese asked Than.

He gave her what seemed an arrogant smirk that said, "Of course."

Before she could ask another question, Than had stripped down to his white boxers and was pulling her into to the frigid water, and she was screaming gleefully again.

"It's so cold!"

"It's awesome," he said. "I've missed you, and all of this, more than you can know."

He held her close, keeping her warm, and was about to kiss her again when they heard the crunch of footsteps along the jetties.

"Pete!" Therese cried, surprised. He had been her rock since last summer, a shoulder to cry on, a friend—maybe more than a friend since Cupid shot his arrow into Pete's heart—to keep her from losing her mind. She pulled back from Than and gave Pete an awkward smile. "Feel like a swim?"

"Hey, Than," Pete said with what seemed like a forced grin. "How's it going?"

"Hey, Pete. How's your family?" Than ran his fingers through his dark wavy hair, maybe in an attempt to appear casual and unaffected by Pete's sudden appearance.

Pete's blond bowl hair cut from last summer had grown out, and he hadn't bothered to cut it. Therese had told him she liked it long. Just now he had it tied back in a ponytail at the nape of his neck. He wore his blue jeans and boots and a long-sleeved shirt open in front, exposing his tanned chest and abdomen. He looked really good, for a mortal.

"The family's okay. Summer is our busy season, you know." Then Pete added, "Need a job?"

"This is a quick visit," Than replied. "But thanks anyway. Tell everybody I said hello."

"You should do it yourself," Pete said. "They'd be happy to see you."

Pete's family—the Holts—ran a trail riding business down the road, and last summer, Than had taken a job as a horse handler when their usual hands had to take time off due to a death in the family. Therese later suspected Than had arranged it all so that they could meet—in the flesh, that is. They had already met when she was in a coma after her parents were killed by one of McAdams's Taliban spies. She had followed her parents to the Underworld, but had assumed it was a dream, and, as she had always been a lucid dreamer and able to manipulate the events of her dreams, she had been especially bossy and flirtatious with the god of death and with his brother, the god of sleep. She couldn't have known then that it had all been real and that the god of death, unused to receiving affection, would fall in love with her and follow her back to the world of the living.

But she was glad. More than glad. She was absolutely thrilled. And now he had finally come back for her. But what would she tell Pete?

She could see the pain in Pete's face.

"Are we still on for the movies tonight?" Pete asked.

Therese could feel the blood leave her face as Than studied it. Surely he, a god, had been aware of her slightly-more-than-friends relationship with Pete. "Umm. I'm not sure, Pete. Can I give you a call?"

Jen stepped up beside Pete with her arms folded across her chest. "Hey, Than. What's up?"

"Hey, Jen. It's good to see you."

Jen, who, like all the people in Therese's life, had remained ignorant of Than's true identity, was pretty steamed that Than hadn't called or written for ten months. Therese also knew Jen wouldn't be too happy that Therese would drop Pete for Than.

3

"It's been a while," Jen said. "I thought maybe, I don't know, you'd fallen off the face of the earth."

"Not exactly," Than said.

"You might have called," Jen said accusingly.

"It's um, complicated."

"Yeah, right. They don't have phones down south in Texas."

"Jen," Therese said sharply. "Give it a rest."

"We're still going to the movies tonight," Jen insisted. "You and me and Pete and Matthew. I already paid for the tickets online and the movie's sold out."

"Take Bobby," Therese said.

Pete clenched his jaw. "Come on, Jen. We've got work to do."

Pete walked away, and when he was out of sight, Jen, who stood there with her arms crossed, said between gritted teeth, "Don't you dare hurt my brother. Our family has been through enough lately. You should know."

Jen referred to the return of her father after three years of estrangement. Therese didn't know the details, but apparently Mr. Holt had hurt Jen in unmentionable ways while drunk, and after years of therapy and being sober, had returned for a second chance. Therese had loaned Jen her invisibility crown, a gift from Artemis, so she could disappear if her father ever fell off the wagon. But Jen had no idea how the crown worked or how it came to be in Therese's possession.

In fact, it was the existence of the crown from Artemis, the locket from Athena, and the traveling robe and gown from Aphrodite that had assured Therese when she was feeling low that the events of last summer hadn't been imaginary.

Before Therese could reply, Than's sister Meg, one of the Furies, appeared beside Jen. She too had her arms crossed, and her blonde hair, blonder and longer than Jen's and curly where Jen's was straight, blew

4

about her face like a gilded sunburst. "This is wrong, Than!" she roared. Her face was pale and her lips bright red, like fresh blood. "You're screwing with the lives of mortals, not to mention the lives of gods."

Jen's mouth dropped open. "What is she talking about, Therese?"

Therese felt her face go white. Why would Meg expose their identity to Jen?

"Back off, Meg!" Than shouted. "This is none of your business."

"Of course it is, dear brother! We are all in danger after the oath we took on the River Styx at Ares's command. Do you wish us all to be ripped apart by the maenads?"

Therese cringed at the memory of Mount Olympus. Therese had broken her deal with the Olympians by refusing to kill McAdams, which would avenge the death of her parents. You couldn't refuse the gods and not face consequences, she supposed.

But Meg's words confused Therese. The maenads, women drunk with the wine of Dionysus, could only rip apart someone who dared rescue Therese from the dead. That's not what Than was doing.

What was he doing, anyway?

Now Tizzie, another of the three Furies, stood beside her sister with her hands on her hips. Her dark, serpentine curls hung loose about her shoulders and caressed the chain of emeralds around her neck. Where her sister was pale like the moon, she was dark like midnight. "Let her go, Than. She's been doing fine with the mortal. Let her live a natural life with Peter Holt."

"Therese, you can't hurt Pete!" Jen shouted. "You just can't!"

"You can't hurt Pete!" the two Furies joined in. Their voices became a chant.

Therese took Than's hand. "Get me out of here," she muttered. "Before they kill me."

5

Suddenly with the sound of an enormous train, the water parted like it must have when Moses commanded the Red Sea.

"What in the world?" Therese stood beside Than, shivering on the rocky bottom.

"Get in!" Poseidon's chariot came out of nowhere, pulled by his three magnificent white steeds, Riptide, Seaquake, and Crest. Poseidon's sun-bleached hair and beard were dry and blowing in the wind against his bronze face, his blue-green eyes scrutinizing them. "What are you waiting for, kids? Get in!"

Than helped Therese into the chariot, and before they had fully sat in the seat beside Poseidon, they were whipped from Lemon Reservoir into the summer sky.

The wind hit Therese's face and stung her now watery eyes. She looked back to see all three Furies following them. Meg and Tizzie were joined by their red-headed sister, Alecto. They were flying through the sky in Hades's chariot, pulled by his two black stallions, Swift and Sure.

Poseidon slapped the backs of his white steeds. "Faster!" he called.

This can't be happening, Therese thought, clinging to Than. The Furies would never reveal themselves to Jen. She gave Than a dubious look. He smiled and kissed her.

Her heart sank in her chest as they soared above the clouds. "Than," she said in his ear. "Tell me this is real!" Despite the threat of the Furies on their tail, she would rather this all be real and her be sitting beside the love of her life than the alternative.

He took her face in his hands and kissed her. She kissed him back longingly. Without letting go of the kiss, she realized the chariot was plummeting, falling back to the earth, to the sea. What sea?

"I wish you'd kiss *me* like that," Hip, Than's brother, the god of sleep, said beside her. He had taken Poseidon's reins.

6

Therese looked at Hip. "What happened to Poseidon?"

"You mean the ugly figment you mistook for Poseidon?"

"No, Hip!" Therese shouted. "This isn't a dream!" She wrapped her arms around Than and buried her face in his fine chest.

"You've gotten better and better at believing in them over these last ten months," Hip said.

"What do you care?" Therese hissed.

"You know the answer to that," Hip said.

"Leave us alone," Than said.

"Shut your figment up," Hip said to Therese.

"He's no figment!"

Hip took out a hand-held mirror and put it up to the three of them. Only two faces gazed back. Than's was invisible.

Therese looked at Than with astonishment. He looked real when she wasn't staring at his absent reflection. He smiled at her, but now that Therese knew for certain he was a disgusting figment, she couldn't bring herself to smile back or to lean in at his attempt to kiss her.

"Figment!" she cried. "I command you to show yourself!"

Than disappeared, and in his place was the laughing eel-like creature. It flitted in the air around them and then flew away. She looked back to see the figments that had once been Furies twirl and sail away, laughing at her.

Therese moaned. "When will he come for me, Hip?"

Hip brushed a strand of his blond wavy hair behind his ear and then pulled back on the reins. He looked a lot like his fraternal twin brother: same awesome golden body and gorgeous blue eyes; but whereas Hip's hair was blond, Than's was dark brown, almost black. Therese had been tempted more than once to give in to Hip's jealous demands for affection. Hip was a womanizer who visited many girls at night in their dreams and had his way with them. Therese had managed to keep him at bay in her own dreams, but it wasn't always easy. He was good at seduction.

"I don't think he ever will," Hip said, pulling hard on the reins but unable to slow the steeds. "It's not his place. He's got a job to do."

"It's not fair," she complained.

"Life isn't fair," Hip smiled. "Only death is. Ask my father. That's his favorite line."

Therese wiped the tears from her eyes and choked down a sob. "You could take me to him," she said with an accusing tone as they continued to plummet toward the sea. "You know you could."

"I've promised him I wouldn't," Hip said. "It would kill you. You already know that. In fact, this conversation is beginning to sound like a scratched up CD that skips back to the same spot."

"Just take me for a moment. I'll leave before I get too weak. Take me once and we'll never talk about this again."

"I swore on the River Styx."

Her eyes widened. "You never told me that before. Why didn't you tell me you swore an oath? I'd have given up by now."

"I tell you in every dream, Therese. You choose not to remember. Now wake up and leave me alone. I've grown tired of your company."

Chapter Two: The Search

Than disintegrated and dispatched to several cities throughout the world, collecting the souls of the dead. The more he disintegrated, the more difficult it was for him to focus on his most important task: finding a way to make Therese his queen. Ares had been clever last summer on Mount Olympus when he'd made them all swear on the River Styx not to make her a god like them, nor were they allowed to retrieve her from the Underworld once she died a mortal death. The situation seemed hopeless, but Than was not without hope. He was determined to find a way.

For the past ten months he had traveled from god to god, taking counsel from all those who would give it. Most of them had urged him to give up his dream of making Therese his wife and queen. They told him love was fleeting, and he would learn to forget her. They said she would be dead within the next eighty years, and this amount of time was but a blink of an eye to a god. Even his own father told him to forget her, saying she wasn't worthy. Hades had gone so far as to force Hip to swear on the River Styx, like the gods on Mount Olympus, never to make Therese a god.

But Aphrodite wept for him and understood his pain. They sat together on Mount Olympus in the banquet hall, alone except for Hestia's coming and goings as she set the table for the next meal. Aphrodite took Than's hand into her own and kissed it, something no god save his mother had ever done.

"I'm so sorry for you," she said softly. "You may not believe this, but I know how you feel. I'm not allowed to be with my true love either."

"Hephaestus isn't your true love?"

9

She pulled her hand away. "Lower your voice." She waited for Hestia to leave the room.

"You knew that, Than. Everyone knows Ares has my heart."

"Then why are you married to Hephaestus?"

"Has it never occurred to you why the most beautiful god would be wed to the only ugly one?"

Than shook his head. "Love is deeper than beauty?"

"God, no." She waved her hand in the air as if to bat such an idea away. "Beauty trumps all, my dear, and Zeus knows that. He feared the people would worship me above him, so he bound me to that hunchback."

"But what good did that do?"

"Beauty also comes from happiness. Some of my beauty faded after my marriage."

"I wouldn't know. I can't imagine you more beautiful."

Aphrodite gave him a smile. "What do you want from me?"

"Can you persuade Ares to change his mind about Therese? Ask him to do it out of love for you?"

"Of course, but that won't help. We've all sworn an oath. Even if Ares sympathizes with your cause, he can't undo what's already been done."

"Does he sympathize?"

"He hates you."

Than was momentarily distracted from the beautiful goddess by the soul of another plant in the hands of a young Indian boy he accompanied to Charon. More and more he was seeing plants evolving souls of their own, like animals and humans. He had been adding these plant souls to his chambers in preparation for the day Therese would join him. He wanted to add as many plants and animals to his chambers as possible for his nature-loving bride-to-be.

Aphrodite touched his hand again and brought his focus back to her. "I'm sorry. Truly. But there's nothing we can do."

"I can't accept that. There's got to be a way. Will you at least think about it, and let me know if an idea comes to you?"

Aphrodite nodded, but her face held no hope.

Then today, months after his conversation with the goddess, Hermes appeared with a summons from Mount Olympus. Aphrodite wished to see him.

Chapter Three: Awake

Therese reached out to Hip but felt something furry in his place. She opened her eyes. She squinted against the bright sun beaming through her bedroom windows. Her eyes gradually adjusted, and she looked around. Her bed covers were thrown across the wooden floor. She lay in her nightshirt, one sock on, one sock off, holding onto her little smooth fox terrier, Clifford. He licked the tears streaming down her cheeks.

"It happened again," she told him. "It seemed so real."

She lay back on her pillow and stared at the ceiling. She noticed a crack that hadn't been there before.

Ten months and not a word from him.

"Than," she whispered. "Thanatos," she said in case his hearing required his full name. "Please do something. Give me a sign you still care about me. I feel so hopeless."

When, once again, nothing earth-shattering happened, she pulled her covers from the floor and lay back down on her bed beneath them. Why get up? What did she have to live for?

"You're so lucky, boy," she said to Clifford. "If only Artemis could have made me immortal when she did it to you. We could be together forever and still have our memories—" Unlike Mom and Dad, she thought, who, because they were dead were forever oblivious to the life they led on earth. They were happy, though, in the Elysian Fields with all of its delusions. It didn't really sound so bad, and was maybe a better alternative to this emptiness and longing she felt ever since their death last year—an emptiness and longing that only worsened when Than came into, and then out of, her life.

She wondered if it would have been better not to have met him at all. She shuddered at the thought. No, better to be miserable.

Then she wondered for the millionth time if she could have possibly imagined it all: meeting the gods of sleep and death, falling in love, receiving magical gifts from goddesses, taking a ride with Poseidon, fighting the man responsible for her parents' death on Mount Olympus and then choosing not to kill him, which meant she could not become a god and join Than in the Underworld forever. She had been in the worst state of depression after her parents' death. Could it have all been a delusion?

No, because of the crown and the robe and the blue dress Aphrodite gave her at the end of the battle on Mount Olympus. Because of the locket from Athena she wore around her neck. They were proof.

Clifford did his I-need-to-go-outside dance, so she climbed from the bed. "Okay, boy. Let's go." She tugged off the one sock and skipped down the stairs.

"Good morning, Sleepyhead," Carol said from the granite countertop where she sipped coffee and read the paper. "It's almost time for swim practice."

"I'm not sure I'm going this morning." She slipped on a pair of flip-flops and then followed Clifford out the back door onto the wooden deck. The screen door slammed shut behind her, so she didn't hear whatever her aunt said next. "Come on, Clifford. Let's go for a walk."

She often walked out in the woods in her nightshirt knowing no one would be around to see her. The Melner Cabin was a half mile away toward the dam (just thinking of last summer's guests in the Melner Cabin made her moan), and the Holts lived three-quarters of a mile on the other side. She had only the deer, the chipmunks, the birds, and the occasional wild horse to contend with, and these companions she gladly welcomed. Just now two chipmunks scurried away from her, and a red bird fluttered beneath the feeder on one of two great elms. She made her wish and blew five kisses before the cardinal could make its escape. She doubted the wish would come true, but it didn't hurt to try.

She looked up at the twin elms, which were both healthy now thanks to her uncle, Richard, who had cut off the diseased branch and had treated the roots of both trees to keep the Dutch elm disease away. He and Carol married last Christmas, and in January Richard's adoption of Therese was finalized. They would now celebrate two birthdays for her: April seventh, the day she was born, and January eighth, the day Richard's adoption of her was official. She had two legal guardians who loved her and took care of her. She had friends who loved her, too. And Pete. Why couldn't this be enough?

"Therese?" Carol called from the back door. "Jen's on her way to pick you up. Better get your suit on."

Therese groaned. "Come on, Clifford. Let's go inside."

Clifford rambled down the trail he and she had made over the years, and together they reentered the house.

"You've missed so much practice," Carol said. "You really need to go today. You're not sick, are you?" Carol's straight red hair was pulled up in a high ponytail and rings of mascara had not yet been washed from her face.

Therese shrugged. "I don't think so. Just tired."

"You're a healthy sixteen-year-old. Why are you so tired all the time? Maybe we should go see Dr. Lanford again."

"I don't like Dr. Lanford, and I don't want to go on Prozac again." The Prozac had interfered with the lucidity of her dreams.

"Maybe a therapist, then. I'll do some research. Your parents have been gone a year. This isn't healthy."

Therese sighed. "I'll go get ready."

She trudged up the stairs, with Clifford at her heels. After she changed into her one-piece, she quickly fed and watered her pets. Puffy

14

still didn't look so good. She suspected he had stayed in his plastic tower all night again. His breathing had been labored for over a week. The vet had said it was time. Four years was a long life for a hamster.

Jewels, her tortoise, had nearly doubled in size since last summer and had required a larger tank. The tank stretched across the expanse of Therese's desk, which was no loss to Therese since she always did her homework on her bed. She stroked the tortoise's shell.

She heard the doorbell, so she slipped on some shorts over her suit, grabbed her bag, and skipped downstairs where she slipped her feet into flip-flops.

"Don't you want some breakfast?" Carol asked.

"Not hungry."

When she opened the door, she found Pete instead of Jen.

"Hey, Therese," he said. "Ready?"

"Where's Jen?"

"In the truck. Hers isn't running so well, and there's no way I'm letting her drive my truck."

"See ya, Carol." Therese followed Pete through the screened front porch and down the steps to the gravelly drive where Jen sat in Pete's truck, waiting.

Jen climbed out of the front bench seat so Therese would sit between her and her brother. Therese wished Jen wasn't pulling so hard for her and Pete to get together—though, in Jen's mind, they kind of already had. Therese now noticed that Jen had dark rings beneath her eyes, and they weren't rings of mascara.

"What's wrong?" Therese asked as Pete backed out of the drive.

"Nothing," Jen said in a way that wasn't convincing.

"Dad got drunk last night. Jen didn't sleep a wink."

"Oh no."

"Yeah," Pete said.

"We don't have to go to practice," Therese offered. "Let's go have breakfast."

Jen shook her head. "I need the practice. I need to get my mind off everything."

"His brother died," Pete explained as he passed Lemon Dam. "He and his brother were close when they were young. Last night was a one-time thing." Then he added, "We hope."

Jen shuddered and Therese could see without looking directly at her that she had started to cry.

"Change the subject," Jen choked out.

Pete and Therese spoke at the same time. Therese said, "How's Matthew?" and Pete said something about his band.

"Go ahead," Pete said.

"No, you go," Therese said.

"Okay. My band is playing in a festival at Pagosa Springs this Saturday night. My whole family is going, I think. I'd love it if you'd come, too."

"Sounds like fun. I'll ask my aunt." She turned to Jen. "Is Matthew going?"

"I think so. Todd and Ray, too."

"Todd and Ray? I haven't seen them since school let out."

"You could ask Vicki, too, if you want," Jen added.

Therese nodded. "Yeah. I should, shouldn't I?"

"It's up to you," Jen replied. "Your call."

Vicki had come to Durango High School half way through their freshman year and had stuck to Therese like glue. She had mousy brown hair and a face that reminded Therese of a Who from Whoville. Therese had tried to be friendly but had felt suffocated by the neediness of the new girl, until the terrible thing happened at the end of the summer: Vicki's mother committed suicide. Therese had made it her mission to get closer

16

to Vicki, and what had started off as charity had gradually grown into a friendship, though still less than equal. Vicki needed Therese and depended on her much more than Therese did Vicki.

"She's coming to the meet," Therese said. "She's coming to support us. She knows how badly I want to beat Lacey Holzmann at breaststroke."

"You should invite her," Pete said. "She's a nice girl."

"Yeah. If my aunt says I can go, I'll give Vicki a ring tonight."

Pete patted Therese's thigh. "Good call."

A slight tingle pulsed up her leg. Pete's strong hand felt good, and despite her nightly rants to Than, Than hadn't contacted her in over ten months. She smiled up at Pete.

"It's not like you're inviting her to prom." Pete laughed.

Prom. She hadn't thought about that, but her junior prom would be coming up this school year in the spring. She knew Pete would go with her if she asked. Should she? Should she really give up on Than?

In fact, Therese couldn't help but suspect Pete had decided not to go to college so he could remain close to her. If Cupid hadn't shot his arrow in Pete's heart, he might be at Colorado State right now. However, Hip did say the arrow only made stronger a feeling already present. How much of Pete's affection for her was real? And if much of it was because of the interference of the gods, did she owe it to Pete to give in to his desires?

Pete pulled into the Durango High Natatorium where a bunch of other cars were already parked. "I'm gonna run some errands. When do I need to be back?"

"Eleven," Jen said as she climbed from the seat. "But it's no big deal if you run late. We can grab a bite at the Subway next door while we wait."

"I'll just meet y'all at Subway, then," Pete said.

17

Therese climbed from the seat and said thanks before closing Pete's truck door. Gina Rizzo was climbing from her Mustang convertible at the same time. Her hair was wrapped into a pretty, neat bun at the nape of her neck, blonde ringlets here and there near her face. Even without makeup, Gina was beautiful—until she spoke. Therese lowered her eyes to avoid her, but it was too late. Gina had seen her and had now caught up to her and Jen.

"Hey, Therese. Hey Jen," she said in a friendly voice. "I heard Lacey's breaststroke has improved by over two seconds since last year. Her cousin is friends with my little sister, you know."

"That's great," Jen said. "Lacey will need those seconds if she wants to come in second to Therese."

Therese gave Jen a grateful glance behind Gina's back.

"Dream on," Gina said in her snotty voice.

They went through the glass doors and into the humid building. Gina skipped ahead of them to avoid whatever Jen would say next.

"Chicken shit," Jen muttered.

When they were away from the other teammates in the locker room putting their things in their lockers before practice, Jen said, "Speaking of prom, Matthew and I are definitely going. I haven't gone shopping for the dress, but I've already found the shoes. They're to die for. You *are* going to ask Pete, aren't you?"

"Jen, it's months away. I haven't given it much thought."

"Well, start giving it some. You can't start shopping too soon."

"Some tomboy you turned out to be."

"Just 'cause I'm good on a horse doesn't mean I can't appreciate pretty stiletto heels."

Therese grabbed her towel from her bag and shut her locker door. "Can you even walk in them?"

"I've been practicing."

18

Therese smiled at the image and wondered if Jen wore the invisibility crown while she practiced so no one would laugh at her. It had to be funny.

They left the locker room together and went to the poolside, where their coach had gathered the rest of their team. Paul caught Therese's eye and licked his lips in an attempt to be sexy. She shuddered. When would he ever get a clue?

Therese was relieved Jen hadn't asked again about Than. For months, she'd say, "Any word from Than?" and Therese's face would turn the color of tomato soup, she'd stop breathing, and she'd nearly faint. She was glad not to have to admit she still hadn't heard anything from the supposed love of her life. She had wanted to lie to her best friend and say, yes, we email all the time, or, I got a letter this afternoon, or, he texted me from Texas yesterday. But she knew her friend would see right through her and know the truth.

The water actually felt good as she warmed up with freestyle. She hadn't come all week—it was Thursday—and she had forgotten how therapeutic it could be. After two laps of freestyle, she switched to back, and then fly, saving her favorite stroke for last. As she swam, she thought of Poseidon's appearance in her dream. It hadn't really been Poseidon, but still, she thought of him. She recalled the ride he had given her on his dolphin, Arion, last summer when he had reluctantly taken her as his prisoner, and then after, on his really cool chariot. "Oh, Poseidon," she prayed silently. "Why won't Thanatos come for me? Should I just go on with my life?"

As if in answer, when she reached the edge of the pool at the end of her twenty-minute warm up and looked up, she saw Pete gazing down at her. "I finished early and thought I'd hang out." He left the poolside and walked over to the stands a few yards away. He looked good in his jeans. He glanced back and caught her watching. She blushed and turned away, but not before catching his wink.

Luckily, the coach called everyone over and lined them up for drills, and she no longer had the luxury—or curse—of thinking.

Chapter Four: Aphrodite's Message

"You can't go like that," Hermes stopped Than before he could god travel to Mount Olympus to answer Aphrodite's summons. "I'm to take your place so you can go in mortal form. She'll meet you at the Café Moulan in Paris near the Louvre. No one's to know of this, not even your father."

Than gave him a grave nod, shook Hermes's hand, and left his position as god of the dead for his rendezvous in Paris, hoping he wouldn't be caught by Hades. His relationship with his father was already strained by the events that took place on Mount Olympus last summer when Therese failed to follow through on her end of the deal she and Hades made with the other gods. Not that Than blamed her. Her compassion for others made her more, not less, desirable to him.

He had forgotten, as he walked the street in Paris, how exhilarating it felt being in mortal form. He could smell the bakery on the corner, feel the sun on his back, and hear the cars passing by and the voices and music carrying out from the shops and cafes with much more intensity than he did as a god, and again he wondered if the lower one went down the animal kingdom, the more intense sensory perceptions became. He wished he could leave his office and join Therese as a man. Life could be so good here on earth with her. But it wasn't to be.

Even in mortal form, Aphrodite was beautiful, though he disagreed that beauty trumped all. As beautiful as Therese was, she couldn't rival a goddess; but it was the whole package that made him love her.

"Please sit," Aphrodite motioned to the chair across from her on the outdoor patio of Café Moulan. She wore a scarf around her head like a hood, whether to protect her face from the afternoon sun or to conceal her identity from others, Than wasn't sure.

"It's good to see you," Than said. "You have some news, I hope?"

"Wine?" She pointed to a glass she had already ordered for him.

Although he had some wine in his rooms, sent to him from Dionysus, he rarely drank. His job required him to have full control of his faculties at all times. He took a sip and closed his eyes.

Aphrodite smiled. "You like?"

"Mmmm." He sipped again. "Yes."

Aphrodite surreptitiously glanced around the patio and then leaned across the table. "Swear on the River Styx you won't tell a soul what I'm about to tell you."

Than returned the glass to the table and lifted his head with surprise. All humor left him as he looked at Aphrodite with wide eyes. "I swear." He felt a mixture of dread and hope as he leaned closer to the goddess to hear what she had to say. Rarely was he asked to take an oath, so he knew this must be important. He hoped it had something to do with a way of making Therese his bride.

"Do you know who's responsible for making wine?"

This question confused Than, not because he didn't know the answer, but because he couldn't fathom how it required such a serious oath. "Dionysus."

"And what do you know of him?"

"He enjoys life. His philosophy is to seize the day and live to the fullest. Wine, good food, dancing, and such are his favorite pastimes, right?"

Aphrodite nodded. "Anything else?"

"He controls the maenads—the wild, frenzied women who tear people's bodies apart. They ripped poor Orpheus to pieces before my

22

eyes. They did leave me a parting gift, though. I have a beautiful sea shell like no other in my room. I also have bottles of his wine, sent to me through Hermes. I've never met him in person, though."

"Do you know nothing more?"

Than shook his head.

"His father?"

"Zeus, I think. Or Hermes? I don't recall."

She took a sip of her wine and then said, "There's a reason you don't."

He leaned closer. "What do you mean?" Had someone put a spell on him?

"The genealogy of Dionysus has been confused for centuries. He is indeed Zeus's son, born of a mortal woman named Semele."

"But how…"

"Not a demigod, I know. Because he was born again of Zeus alone."

"I don't understand."

"Hera got wind of the affair and tricked Semele into asking Zeus to swear to grant her a wish. He swore on the River Styx. But her request was to see him in his full godly form, which as you know, is too bright for human eyes. But he had sworn, so even though he knew it would kill her, he showed himself to her."

"How awful."

"Indeed." She took another sip of her wine. "As Semele died, she gave birth prematurely to Dionysus. Zeus cut a hole in his thigh and placed the unformed infant there, stitching him in until he was ready to be born. Because Dionysus was later born solely to Zeus, immortality was conferred onto him."

"But I thought Dionysus's mother was also immortal. Is that a lie?"

Aphrodite shook her head. "He went back to the Underworld, this was back in Hermes's day, when he used to ferry the dead, when you and Hip were still too young."

"What does all of this have to do with me?"

"Because Dionysus spends his time partying in the mountains with the maenads and the nymphs and the satyrs, many people, and even some gods, think he's this lesser goat-like god who has very little power and authority on Mount Olympus."

"But that's not true?"

"No." Aphrodite glanced around the café. Then her eyes fell on something across the patio. "Oh no."

"What's wrong?"

"It's Ares. He's looking for me. We have an apartment here in Paris. I didn't know where else to meet you. Let's leave before he discovers us talking. There's too many around for god travel. Follow me."

Than followed her from the patio to a lime green Lamborghini parked a block away—not exactly inconspicuous.

"Get in."

He climbed inside behind the wheel.

"Drive!" Aphrodite commanded.

Than gaped. He had no idea how. "I've never driven a car before."

"You're kidding me."

"Tell me when I would have the time. You others have no idea what kind of life I lead."

"Switch places with me." They vanished and reappeared in the opposite seats. Aphrodite turned the key in the ignition and pulled the car away from the curb, causing him to fall back and shriek. "Strap yourself in!"

Than looked around and fumbled with the harness as Aphrodite darted past cars, coming close to crashing several times. He wasn't afraid of death—he was death, after all—but he was afraid of extreme pain, something he'd only experienced a few times in his long life.

"Pull over!" he shouted.

"Hold on!" She made a sharp turn and led him down an alley, where she slowed down the car and came to a stop. "I think I lost him, but we have to make this quick. He'll soon trace my scent."

"You were saying Dionysus is a more formidable god than most realize."

"Exactly. People confuse him with Pan, and rightly so, because Pan doesn't exist."

"What?" Than searched Aphrodite's profile for signs of mockery. "Are you kidding? How can that be?"

"You've heard the rumors he's dead?" She made another sharp turn.

"He's not in the Underworld."

"After Dionysus was born, Zeus put him in Hermes's care to protect him from Hera. When dressing him as a girl didn't keep him from Hera's suspicion, Hermes turned him into a goat and named him Pan and raised him as his own son. The stories of the two became convoluted over time, and intentionally so, to protect Dionysus."

"And this concerns me because..."

"Because unlike all of the other powerful gods of Mount Olympus, he did not swear an oath on the River Styx never to make Therese immortal."

Tears fled to Than's mortal eyes and startled him. As a god, he could shed tears, but as a man, they felt different. He looked into Aphrodite's beautiful face, wanting to kiss her with joy. "Thank you. I can't thank you enough."

"Not so fast," Aphrodite frowned.

"What?"

"In order to ask Dionysus to help you, you will need to win his favor. But first, you will need to make it past the maenads. They'll want to rip you apart."

Chapter Five: Surprise

Friday morning, Jen picked up Therese in her own truck—Pete stayed behind—and before Therese had climbed into the vehicle, Jen said, "My family has a surprise for you. You have to come over today right after practice."

"What is it?" Therese asked.

"It's a surprise. I can't tell you."

All through practice, Therese wondered what the surprise could be. Were they going to offer her a summer job? Had Mrs. Holt made her another jar of tomato jelly (which she loved)? Was Pete going to ask her to prom? Her stomach churned with anticipation.

During the ride back, Therese asked for a hint. "Come on," she begged. "Just a little one?"

"It's bigger than a bread box."

Okay, at least that ruled out a jar of tomato jelly.

When they arrived at the Holts, the first trail rides of the day had already begun, but Mrs. Holt had stayed behind and was waiting near the pen.

It must be a summer job, Therese thought with dread as she walked toward Mrs. Holt. Therese hadn't been on a horse since Dumbo's accident, and she hadn't groomed the horses much since, either.

"Mornin' Therese," Mrs. Holt said. "Well, I guess it's almost noon. You want some lunch?" Her blonde hair was mostly gray and cut like a bowl around her thin, leathery, freckled face.

"No thank you," Therese replied.

"Let's show her the surprise!" Jen said.

"Well Pete and Bobby wanted to be here, too, but I guess Jen can't wait to show you. Let's go inside the barn."

Therese followed Mrs. Holt into the barn, fresh and clean from this morning's chores, to a back stable and pointed to a newborn gray foal in a stall with Sassy.

"That's Sassy's colt," Mrs. Holt explained. "Dumbo was his father."

The foal lay close to his mother, eyeing Therese suspiciously.

"But how? That was over ten months ago." Dumbo was spooked by a snake last summer and broke two legs and had to be put down.

"Horses gestate for eleven months," Mrs. Holt said softly. "Sassy was pregnant before the accident."

Therese looked again at the little gray foal. "What's his name?"

"We're waiting for you to name him," Mrs. Holt said. "This here colt belongs to you, young lady. He's a gift from the family, if you want him, that is."

Therese's mouth dropped open. Just then, Bobby and Pete scrambled in from the pen.

"You've already told her?" Bobby complained. "We wanted to be here, Mama."

Therese couldn't believe how tall Bobby had gotten since school let out three weeks ago. He was almost as tall as Pete now, but, unlike his brother, had kept the boyish bowl haircut, though now it was covered with a white cowboy hat.

"I just told her, Bobby. She hasn't even answered yet. What do you say Therese?"

Jen nudged her friend. "Speechless?"

Therese nodded as the tears rolled down her cheeks. First she hugged Jen, then Mrs. Holt, then Bobby, and finally, Pete, who held onto her longer than the others.

Pete chuckled when he released her. "I think that's a yes," he said.

Therese went over to the newborn colt, which lay in the hay. Sassy stood behind him, her teats full of milk.

"How old is he?" Therese asked.

"Two days," Pete and Jen said together.

"May I pet him?"

Mrs. Holt came up beside her. "He's still getting used to being handled, so for now, use a flat hand at his tail head, just here." Mrs. Holt took Therese's hand and guided it to the top of the colt's tail.

The colt moved his tail closer to Therese.

"I think he likes it," Therese said, smiling. She reached out and stroked the tail head again.

"Now try gently scratching," Mrs. Holt encouraged.

The colt moved closer to Therese, and Sassy put her head nearby to get a better view of what was going on.

"It's okay, Sassy," Pete said, stroking the mare. "It's okay, girl."

"So what are you going to name him?" Bobby asked.

"I'm not sure. He looks like a little gray cloud." *Cloudy? Foggy? Tornado? Thundercloud? Thunderhead? Cumulus—is that the scientific name for thunderhead? Hmm, Thunderbolt?* Then it came to her. "Stormy. I'll call him Stormy."

"Perfect!" Jen said.

"But is he really mine?"

"Well, Hon', obviously you can't take him home," Mrs. Holt replied. "You'll have to keep him here. But he's yours to take care of, if you want him, and when he's older, you can pay me back for his keep by letting me trail ride him in the summers. I'll cover all his expenses. You just take care of him. You'll have to ride him when he's old enough. It's up to you. It's a big responsibility, so you might want to think about it. You have to come at least twice a week to get him used to you and used to grooming."

29

Jen put her hand on Therese's shoulder. "Mom thought it might help you want to be with the horses again. You haven't been around them much. They miss you."

The colt nuzzled Therese's hand, and that sealed the deal. "You're so cute, Stormy. Such a cute little fella. I love you so much."

Pete laughed. "I think he loves you, too."

Therese felt the blood rush to her cheeks. Pete might have said, "I think I love you, too," the way her body had responded. But he hadn't. Of course he hadn't. He was talking about Stormy.

"This is such a wonderful gift," Therese said. "I'll have to talk with my aunt and uncle, I suppose."

"I already done cleared it with them, Hon'," Mrs. Holt said. "But you take some time to think on it."

Mr. Holt walked into the barn. "The next group has arrived," he said. Then he noticed Therese with the colt. "So what do you think, Therese? He's perty, ain't he?"

"Very perty," she agreed.

"Named him yet?"

"Stormy," Bobby said. "She's decided to name him Stormy."

"Well that sounds about right," Mr. Holt laughed, "considering the way he came into this world kickin' and a fussin'."

"I wish I could have been there," Therese said.

"None of us were," Pete said. "Dad's just makin' that up."

"No, son, I was here. That was the night I heard the news about Jim. Jim was my brother, Therese. I passed—I mean fell asleep out here in the barn drownin' my sorrows. I locked myself in here so I wouldn't…wake any of you. Stormy here woke me up about four a.m. as he came into the world."

The group fell silent, and Therese continued to scratch Stormy all around his rump. Sassy's snort broke the silence.

"I expect she wants to nurse," Mrs. Holt said. "And the second group is waiting. Better get on it, boys."

As Pete headed toward the barn door, he turned and asked Therese, "You comin' tomorrow night to the festival?"

"Oh, you gotta come!" Bobby said, ahead of his brother.

"I'm planning on it," Therese said.

Pete gave her a smile and then disappeared from the barn.

Saturday morning, during warm up, something strange flickered just below the surface of the water where Therese swam freestyle. Rather than turning at the wall, she stopped, grabbed another breath, and pressed her face down to take a look. Before the image came into view, she thought it was someone's towel that had fallen in by accident, but as the image floated toward her from the depths, she nearly sucked in water because of the shock. It was Poseidon's face—not his whole body—looking up at her. She brought her head up and looked around at the other swimmers. Jen was swimming backstroke in the lane beside her. Carol, Richard, Vicki, and the Holts were up in the stands. Therese dug her finger beneath the swim cap to unclog an ear, grabbed another gulp of air, and thrust her face back down into the water. Poseidon spoke, and, oddly, she could hear him perfectly.

"I have heard your prayers, and although I cannot offer you Thanatos or save your pet, I can help you beat your opponent. As I control all the waters of the Earth, I can command this small pool to make you the winner of your entire swim meet. Do you desire this of me?"

Therese lifted her head from the water, shook it several times to clear the water from her ears. She saw Gina Rizzo swimming butterfly two lanes down. Jen called over from the lane next to her.

"Everything alright?"

Therese nodded. Then she thrust her head back into the water. Poseidon had disappeared.

"No, Poseidon," Therese blubbered into the water, in case she hadn't imagined him. "I want to win this on my own. But thanks, anyway."

His face reappeared. "As you wish." Then he vanished again.

Therese pulled her head up. Gina smirked at her through the water as she came up to breathe during the fly, causing Therese to have second thoughts about her answer to Poseidon.

"What are you doing?" her coach called from above. "Lose something down there?"

Therese blushed as she looked up at her balding coach and his puzzled face.

"I thought I saw a pair of goggles down there, but it's nothing."

"Finish this lap and climb on out," the coach said. "We're about to start."

Despite the humidity and the heat in the high school natatorium, Therese shivered on the bench beneath her towel as she waited with her teammates to swim in her events. Her goggles were perched on her head over her swim cap, and she bounced her knees alternately, full of nerves. She looked around at the banners and decorations that were only up for meets. The natatorium had transformed.

This would be her first meet since her parents' death—the first meet of her life they wouldn't be in attendance, because the swim team at Durango High was part of a summer-only league. Across the pool, she could see her aunt and uncle sitting beside Vicki and the entire Holt clan—including Mr. Holt—in the stands behind them. She could tell from the way they had all been treating her that they knew what she was thinking: *My parents aren't here. For the first time in my life, they won't see me race.* Pete noticed she was looking his way and gave her a thumbs up. She returned the gesture with a meek, nervous smile.

Why hadn't she accepted Poseidon's help?

Jen, who sat beside Therese, handed over a green sharpie so Therese could record her event, heat, and lane numbers on the top of her thigh rather than trying to memorize them. When she finished copying from the heat sheet, which Jen had held out for her, she handed the sharpie over, and her knees resumed their nervous bouncing.

"Thanks," Therese said.

"You want me to write 'Eat my bubbles' on your back?" Jen asked.

"Sure."

"Do me first."

The night before, Therese had prayed to all the gods except Ares to save Puffy, bring back Thanatos, and help her team win the meet. She hadn't expected anyone to actually materialize and answer her. The appearance of Poseidon had her so distracted that she messed up the words on Jen's back. She had written "Eat my" so big, that there wasn't much room left for "bubbles." Knowing Jen, she'd check herself out in the locker room mirror. Therese decided to draw the bubbles. The finished product actually looked pretty cool.

During the relay, she could hear her family and friends cheering her on as she pulled and kicked, pulled and kicked the breaststroke. When she neared the end of the lane, she reached out to touch the wall with both hands so Jen could finish with fly. There was something wrong with the wall, though. It had become a spongy mucky mess. Before she had time to think, her hands slipped through the wall of the pool, and her whole body followed.

She found herself in a puddle of mud.

"Climb out and wash off. You're a mess," a voice called.

Therese wiped the mud from her goggles with her fingers and looked up. Above her stood a beautiful young woman with flowing brown hair and high brown suede boots. Therese removed her goggles to get a better look.

"Come on!" the woman urged her. "You're a filthy mess. Take this towel."

"Artemis?" she asked, scrambling to her feet. She took the towel and wiped her face. Immediately the mud left her body and one-piece swimsuit, and she was clean all over. The white towel showed no trace of dirt.

"Of course."

"I'm, I'm supposed to be racing right now."

"It'll wait. No worries. I have something important to tell you." She didn't look back at Therese as she made her way through the woods.

"Where are we going?" Therese followed, slowly because of her bare feet. The dead leaves and twigs scratched at her sensitive skin.

"Just through here."

After another ten feet or so, they came to a small clearing where there were two tree stumps, side by side.

"Sit down," Artemis said as she sat on one of the two stumps.

Therese sat on the other and looked up at Artemis expectantly.

"I've heard your prayers and have decided you need a personal response. First, as to your pet hamster, there's something you need to understand about immortality." The wind gently blew Artemis's brown hair across her green eyes, and she swiped it from her face with a strong hand. "Not all creatures would benefit from it, especially rodents. Your hamster's life consists of feeding, sleeping, and toiling, and that's it. To extend such a life infinitely would be a cruel punishment, not unlike that of Sisyphus, who, at the break of each dawn, rolls the same large rock up the same steep hill. Do you understand?"

Therese thought on it for a moment. Were some lives more valuable than others, or more worthy of living? She wasn't sure of the answer, but she gave Artemis a nod. Maybe Puffy had had enough. "I suppose it would be selfish of me."

Artemis smiled. "Yes. Quite."

Therese shivered. She thought she could see a line of ants marching their way up the stump upon which she sat, and she was cold and worried about the swim meet.

"Immortality would be cruel for most creatures, including most humans. Death in the Elysian Fields is a gift, not a curse, from the gods. Which leads me to another of your prayers—your request for Thanatos."

Therese gave Artemis her full intention, even as another shiver made its way down her back. "Yes. I love him," she said, just above a whisper.

Artemis rolled her eyes and shook her head. "I beseech you to let that go, child. Love is fleeting. And life in the Underworld would be, well, gruesome. It's a place avoided by all gods who *can* avoid it. Even Persephone..."

"Forgive me, Artemis, but I don't care. I love Thanatos, and I want to be with him forever." A flurry of fear moved through Therese as she watched Artemis's green eyes glare back.

"Then you're doomed to heartbreak until the love wears off, which will happen, I assure you, since Cupid never speared your heart. Why any woman would give her heart away, I know not!"

Therese gave into the shivers overtaking her body. She hugged the towel around her and tucked her chin down to her chest.

"If it weren't for your valiant fighting on Mount Olympus last summer, not to mention your selfless decision to give your friend the invisibility crown, I would call you a stupid, stupid girl. Your decision to let McAdams live was noble in the eyes of some, but your foolish,

35

unrelenting desire to be with the god of death is despicable. Yet you remain a good steward of the earth and its inhabitants, and your good-natured, competitive spirit in the water is admirable. Leave me now with the wisdom I've imparted to you, and know I can answer the last of your three requests: you will win your races today."

Therese resisted the urge to object. She had already angered Artemis enough. Her refusal to accept her help in the swim meet would likely sever their ties completely.

"Thank you," Therese said.

"Go! Go!" Artemis shouted angrily.

Therese was bewildered. She didn't know the way back.

"Go!" Artemis shouted again.

Therese scrambled from the tree stump and stumbled on the dead leaves and twigs back toward the mud puddle. It had been somewhere here, just past this clearing, somewhere here in the thick of the woods. She tripped on a heavy branch and fell.

"Go!" she heard the crowd shouting above her.

She found herself back in the pool, reaching for the wall beneath Jen's feet with both hands. She touched the wall, and Jen dove over her head and swam the butterfly to finish the race.

Her relay team came in first.

Therese won every one of her events.

The Durango Demons were declared the winners of the meet.

After the initial excitement and flood of pride, Therese sat on the bench with her handful of ribbons feeling dissatisfied. Artemis's help had ruined her chances of knowing for certain whether or not she could have outswam Lacey Holzmann on her own. As she watched her teammates congratulating one another with hugs and pats on the back, she fought the frustration clutching at her insides. Then suddenly, the ground below her shifted and she half-expected to come face-to-face with another god.

The building shook, and the crowd of people screamed and began to scatter. She sat there on the bench, stunned as she watched her teammates run for their loved ones. Coolers of water fell over, clip boards dropped from tables, chairs were toppled, and people slipped on the wet deck. A crack ran up the cement wall across from her.

Suddenly someone grabbed her arm and pulled her up and away from the water.

"The locker rooms are safest," Richard said beside her.

"This way," Carol said.

And so Therese followed her aunt and uncle and the rest of the panicked crowd into the locker rooms until the earthquake ended and they were finally able to leave the building and go home.

Chapter Six: Hermes's Advice

Than returned to the Underworld to his private chambers to find Hermes lying on his bed.

"Thank god." Hermes sat up. "I'd forgotten what monotonous work this is. I'm in four thousand different places at once and still bored. Take my hand before I'm forced to disintegrate again."

Than touched his cousin's hand and restored himself as god of death, the transition momentarily jostling the lifeless souls he now stood beside, leading them, his hand paternally on their shoulders, to Charon. He sighed. Hermes was right, but someone had to do it. He turned to his cousin. "Thank you."

"Good news from Aphrodite, I hope?"

"An idea. How well do you know Dionysus?"

"He's like a son to me. Why?"

"What can I do to get on his good side?"

"You can't."

Than took a chair across from Hermes, who remained sitting on the bed and now tucked a pillow under his arm to make himself more comfortable. "Why not?"

"He hates the gods. All of us. He feels cheated. And rightly so. He was hidden away most of his life from Hera. You know the story?"

Than nodded. "But I had nothing to do with it."

"He's got a chip on his shoulder. Don't take it personally."

"There's got to be a way. He's my only hope."

"If he's your only hope, then you have none."

"Is it true he lives on Mount Kithairon?"

"Don't seek him out. The maenads will tear you to pieces."

Than bit his lip, thinking. There had to be a way into Dionysus's heart. Every person was capable of tenderness. As god of the dead, he'd seen even the most powerful weep. "How long does it take to recover from that—being torn to pieces?"

"Trust me when I say nothing is worth that pain. Don't even think of it."

"Too late, Hermes." The pain in his heart was greater; he was sure of it.

"First love. Young love. Believe me, it'll pass."

"Impossible. And I don't want it to pass. You know how monotonous my existence is. Why shouldn't I find happiness? Why should I alone be exempt from it?" He thought of Charon and clenched his jaw. Charon, too, was exempt.

"You have nothing he desires. No leverage. He celebrates life. You are Death. I can think of nothing to help you. And as far as how long it takes to put your pieces back together again? Depends on how badly you're ripped apart. Could take weeks. And you'll need help if you don't want to look like a monster for several years while you heal. Plus, someone else would need to take your job while you're put back together, and it won't be me, cousin." Hermes stood up, as if to leave, but then added. "But there is one among us he respects."

"Who?"

"Your grandmother, Demeter. Maybe she can help." With that, Hermes vanished.

Chapter Seven: Vicki's Idea

"But what magnitude are they saying it was?" Richard asked Carol from behind the wheel of his black Maxima. "I don't see any damage anywhere else. It's like it just hit the one building."

"Maybe they don't know yet," Therese said in the backseat with Vicki on their way to Vicki's apartment. Therese had changed from her swimsuit, and, though her hair was still damp, it had been freed from the swim cap and brushed out in the locker room before they left the meet.

"I'm searching," Carol said, bent over her iPhone. "The reception slows down when we get into the pines. Hang on. Okay. Here it is. Five point zero. Wow. Pretty decent."

"Coach said we'll have to use another pool for the rest of the season," Therese said. "I wonder where that'll be."

Richard shook his head. "Five point zero. That is something. Most of the earthquakes in this area hover below three and are rarely felt. I wonder if more will follow. They usually do when they're that big. I wrote an article on earthquakes once."

Therese wondered if Poseidon had been involved. Maybe he was peeved Artemis had helped Therese after Therese had turned down his offer. Surely he knew it hadn't been Therese's fault. Before she had time to think more on it, though, Vicki whispered something cryptic in her ear.

"What?" Therese whispered back.

"I saw my mom last night."

Therese looked at her friend for a moment, wondering what she could mean. Then she asked, "In a dream?"

Vicki gave an even wider smile at Therese's confusion. "Not a dream. Come over for lunch and I'll tell you all about it."

Therese felt wiped out after the meet and the bizarre earthquake, not to mention her unexpected encounters with two gods. She really wanted to go home and take a nap before the festival tonight. But there was something bewildering about Vicki's smile and her apparent certainty that she had seen her mother, who committed suicide a year ago. Therese couldn't resist.

"Hey," she said to her aunt and uncle when there seemed a pause in their conversation about all the seismic occurrences in the history of the planet Earth. "Can I stay at Vicki's for a while?"

Carol turned and looked at Therese. "You don't want to get some rest before tonight?"

"Just a couple of hours," Therese said. "Maybe you could come back for me around three?"

Vicki said, "My dad can bring you home. He won't mind."

"Are you sure?" Carol gave Therese a scrutinizing look. She was aware of the inequity in the relationship between the two girls.

Therese nodded. "Absolutely. Jen's not picking me up until six. I'll have plenty of time to rest."

"What do you think?" Carol asked Richard.

"Fine with me. If Vicki's dad can't bring you home, just give us a call. I've got some errands to run, so I don't mind coming back to town."

Therese hoped Carol wouldn't bring up the fact that Therese was old enough to take driver's education and drive herself, and that her brand new shiny red Honda Civic was waiting in the driveway for her use. Carol had brought it up many times, but Therese hoped she wouldn't in front of Vicki.

The car had been a gift from Carol and Richard last April on her sixteenth birthday, but ever since what happened in her mother's car last summer, Therese could not bring herself to get behind a wheel. At first, Carol and Richard assumed Therese's hesitance had to do with the fact that she didn't want to drive her father's truck. They originally planned for Therese to use it. But when they traded in the truck and bought her a brand new car, Therese still felt like she wasn't ready to drive.

"Some people take longer than others to feel ready," Therese had said.

That had been three months ago, and today Therese didn't feel any more ready to learn to drive.

Vicki lived on the northern outskirts of Durango in a second story apartment with scenic mountain views. Therese had only visited two other times, both since Mrs. Stern's death, and both times the place had been in disarray. Today was no different. As soon as they entered the apartment and stepped into the living room, Therese recognized the pile of clean laundry that seemed always to occupy the dining room table, and closet doors to the washer and dryer stood open with more laundry, presumably dirty, spilling out from on top of the machines and onto the floor. Therese thought the location of the laundry closet was a major flaw in the design of the apartment, because the position from the dining room table was the only one, except for the balcony, offering the spectacular views that made these apartments worth living in. Their exterior was not quite shabby, but certainly left something to be desired with its dull dirty white siding and lack of nearby garden. The views of the mountains *made* the apartments, but unfortunately, the views in the Stern apartment were thwarted by the inefficient laundry system overtaking the best square footage. Therese wondered if things had been different when Mrs. Stern was still living here.

On the other side of the laundry heap, Mr. Stern stood stirring something on the stove.

"Hey, Dad," Vicki called as they crossed into the small galley kitchen. "I hope it's okay if Therese stays for lunch. Whatcha cooking?"

"Oh, hi Therese." Mr. Stern was tall and thin, and the thin white muscle shirt showed just how gaunt with the ruffle of ribs pressing through the material. His plaid shorts hung loose and reached down to his knobby knees and bony legs, which seemed less hairy to Therese than her own had been before she had started shaving. Despite the lack of hair on his legs, the mousy brown hair on his head was long and stringy and looked in need of washing. "We're always glad for the company. I'm just making some chicken noodle soup. It's from a box. Hope that's okay with you girls."

"Smells good," Therese said.

Mr. Stern had retired from the Air Force the year the Sterns moved to Durango. He had taken a part-time job at Fort Lewis College teaching computer science and was off for the summer. Therese suspected money was tight in the Stern household. The worn-out furniture and near bare pantry were only a couple of things giving her that impression.

They took their bowls out to the balcony where there was no table, but where there were three Adirondack chairs. Therese wondered if she were sitting in Mrs. Stern's chair as she and Mr. Stern sat on either side of Vicki.

Vicki and Therese told Mr. Stern all about the meet and the earthquake. He said he hadn't felt anything, but he was always interested in earthquakes, so as soon as they finished their soup, he went to the living room and turned on the television to the local news hoping to hear more about the disturbance. He also went to the computer on the small desk near the television and searched the web for news. Therese thanked him for the soup and then followed Vicki to her room.

The girls sat on either side of Vicki's bed—there was no other seating in the room, and only one other piece of furniture: an old, dusty dresser with a mirror hanging over it. Vicki's clothes were scattered on the floor. Therese wondered how she could have enough clothes to overtake the dining room, laundry closet, and the floor of her bedroom. At least the bed was made, which Therese found rather strange. Why make the bed if the rest of the room was so messy?

Therese had just begun to suspect she had been tricked into coming for a visit when Vicki asked, "Have you ever heard of NDE drugs?"

Therese shook her head, disappointed that Vicki was going in a drug direction. Therese had warned Vicki to stay away from the "Demon Druggies" at school, but she had noticed Vicki sometimes talked to them in a friendly way. She dreaded what Vicki might say next.

"Near death experience. The scientific name is ketamine."

Therese's heart rate picked up. "What do you mean 'near death'?"

"Something happens when you take the drug that causes you to die for a few minutes. Then the drug wears off and you come back to life."

"You *die* for a few minutes? Isn't that risky?"

"Therese, I've been to the other side. I saw my mom."

"You're joking."

"I've never been more serious in my life. Do you want to hear about it or not?"

Therese shifted on the bed. "I'm listening."

"Okay, so last night after my dad went to bed, I injected myself with the ketamine, okay? About five or ten minutes later, I had this awesome feeling of peace. I haven't felt that way since before my mother died. It was so weird, actually, to feel that good, that content. That feeling alone makes me want to do it again."

Therese was growing impatient. "So what happened?"

"Okay, so I'm lying right here on my bed, just like this." Vicki moved over and lay on her pillow on her back. "Then I swear I had this feeling like I was leaving my body. I flew right up there," she pointed to the ceiling in the corner of the room, "and I hovered there for a while— I'm not sure how long. I could literally see myself down here lying on the bed."

"And?"

"Okay, so I'm floating outside of my body, and then it's like the lights go out. I'm somewhere dark, like in a tunnel, and I can see this light at the end. As I go through the tunnel, there's all this fog all around me, and when I get to the end, I see this enormous body of water, like a lake or a river or something."

Therese felt a shudder move down her back. "And then?"

Vicki sat back up. "So then I see this thing like a raft, and on board is this old man. He looks at me all surprised, like he's not expecting me. He doesn't say anything to me. He just stares at me, like he's checking me out. I'm afraid to speak, so I just stand there staring back at him. After a while, I look back behind me, and I can no longer see my room or my body lying on the bed. So I turn back to the old man and say, 'Can you take me across?'

"He doesn't answer, so I wait. Then I just decide to step aboard. The raft man starts pulling us across with this long pole, and I'm so happy and peaceful because I feel sure I'm going to see my mom. It's so strange how I wasn't frightened at all."

Therese's heart was racing. "Then what happened?"

"We floated past these three big black dogs—I think there were three, the fog was so thick I could barely see two feet in front of me. And then there was this huge black iron gate that creaked as it opened. On the other side there was this cavern and inside were three strange-looking people kind of floating just above the surface of the water. They wore long white robes, unlike the filthy red one of my raft man, and they looked clean, but kind of strange, and they pointed the raft man to take me

45

down one of three paths. I could see the light getting brighter and brighter from a river of fire as we wound round the water in through the foggy cavern.

"The raft fell down some rapids, but I wasn't scared—it was fun, actually—and then we went deeper and deeper away from the bright light into darkness. Someone was holding a lantern at the bottom. There were people lying comfortably in a shallow pool of water, like they were sunbathing in the darkness. I saw my mom sprawled out with her eyes closed, and she was still wearing the dress we buried her in. She was beside this really enormously fat dude, but she didn't seem to notice or care about him. Before I could cry out her name, before she could open her eyes to see me, the raft started moving backward. The old raft man looked at me with a threatening glare, like he had known all along I wasn't supposed to be there and his suspicions were now somehow confirmed. There was yelling coming from above. I thought I heard someone yell, 'Grab her!' but then I had left the raft and was flying away from the river back through a dark tunnel. Then I was at my ceiling looking down at my body. All at once I opened my eyes and I was here, again, in my own body, right here on my bed."

Therese stared at her, speechless.

"So what do you think? You believe me, don't you?"

The details of Vicki's tour through the first part of the Underworld were too like what she herself had seen. Therese gave a nod. "I think so. That's so, so weird."

"Yes, it was. Next time I won't wait so long to get on the raft. I think that's why I ran out of time."

"Next time? You mean, you're going to do it again?"

"Of course. Why wouldn't I?"

"Where did you get the drug?"

Vicki's eyes beamed. "Okay, you have to promise not to tell a soul, do you hear me? Not a soul!"

"I promise."

"I swear, if you tell anyone, I'll be so hurt, Therese. It'll be like my mom dying all over again. I won't be able to take it."

"I get it. I promise not to tell."

"Okay, so you know Raleigh Jones?"

"The senior at our school?"

"Yeah. He waits tables at the Ranch House Restaurant down the road from here. My dad and I, we rarely go out to eat, but it would have been my mom's birthday, and we needed a pick-me-up, you know? So a week ago we went, and Raleigh was our waiter, and it turns out it was his birthday, too. Anyway, he was giving away gifts, mostly to the other waiters and waitresses and the bartenders, but he recognized me, and so he brought me one, too, this silly little frog." She held up a frog stuffed animal. "He said it was from the Dollar Store—that all his gifts were—but that's how he celebrated his birthday every year. He bought a bunch of funny stuff from the Dollar Store and handed it out to his friends."

"That's nice."

"That's what I said. I told him he was supposed to receive gifts, not give them away, on his birthday. My dad told him about it being my mom's birthday, and of course he knew what happened—everyone knows—and so that's when he invited me to come to his house later for a party.

"I guess my dad was just glad a boy was showing interest, so he didn't seem bothered by the fact that the party wouldn't start until almost midnight, because that's how long it would take Raleigh to close down his station at the restaurant. Raleigh asked if I wanted to wait at the bar till he got off. I could drink free sodas..."

"Sodas?"

47

"I mean pop. You all call them pop, I forgot. Anyway, and then he'd take me to the party. He said he'd have me home by two o'clock, if that was alright."

"My aunt says sodas, too. So, you're dad let you stay out till two in the morning?"

"My dad was never a stickler with rules. I've never really had a curfew, though up till then, I'd never gone out late. Besides you, well, I haven't made many friends here yet, and after what Mom did, well, I think people are afraid of me or something."

"It just takes time."

"I know. Anyway, so I had a blast at his party. People were smoking pot and taking other stuff, too, but I just drank soda, I mean pop. Then a couple of people came running in from his bedroom—it's just his granny living with him and she's practically deaf. His mom died three years ago and his dad split when he was born. Anyway, this couple runs in, they're seniors, too, one's a football player, I think, and they say they've just come back from the dead. So they tell their story. They've seen their loved ones and stuff. A few days later, I call Raleigh and ask how I can have a near death experience, too. So he gets me the ketamine. And now you know the whole story."

Therese filled with inexplicable excitement. "Do you think he could get me some, too?"

Vicki smiled. "I thought you might be interested. I thought maybe next time I try it, we could do it together, you know?"

Therese nodded. "Yes. Let's do. But isn't it risky? I mean, has anyone actually stayed dead?"

"I did a whole bunch of research before I did it, Therese. Out of the thousands of cases, a few have gone wrong, but the researchers attribute it to something avoidable—like the subject took too much of the drug, or inhaled a powder form rather than injected a liquid, or did

48

consecutive doses, and stuff like that. I think as long as you do the right dose, inject it in liquid form, and wait at least a week in between episodes, it's really safe."

Therese would do her own research, but in the meantime, she'd go ahead and plan this thing with Vicki. Maybe there was a way she could actually see her parents. Certainly she would see Than, wouldn't she? She could plead with him to come back for her, or to at least let her know how much longer he thought it would be before they could be together again. "So next weekend, will you be ready?"

"I'll have to get more from Raleigh. It costs money, though."

"How much?"

"Fifty bucks a pop. Raleigh gave me the first dose for free, but he says he'll have to charge me next time. It's expensive stuff and hard to get. And right now lots of people are into it."

"I can pay for both of ours. I have a lot of money saved up. I'll give you the money tonight at the festival."

"Oh, the festival! That's right! We need to get you home so you can rest. It's almost three." Vicki jumped up and Therese followed her out of the room.

During the car ride home, the two girls talked some about what they were going to wear that night and when Matthew was supposed to be by to pick up Vicki. Matthew was going to drive Vicki, Therese, and Jen. Pete would have to go early in his own truck to set up his equipment with the rest of his band. Mr. and Mrs. Holt would drive Bobby out there in their truck. Todd and Ray would meet them all there, too.

Once the details were worked out and the girls grew quiet, Therese thought about the NDE drug and the possibility of seeing her parents and Than. She was excited, though a little frightened. She would definitely have to do some research first. But so what if she did die? She'd be with him and her parents and untie the lonely knot in her gut.

She'd rather go as a god, of course, but the risk seemed worth taking. Besides, Vicki had said only a few had died and the researchers believed the deaths had been avoidable.

Therese went straight to her room after saying hi to Carol and Richard. She checked on her pets. She turned off Jewel's lamp and wished the tortoise a good night. Puffy still didn't look so good. She gingerly took him from his tower—she knew it was selfish of her, for the vet had said to leave him alone and just keep him comfortable, but Therese felt the need to kiss him and tell him she loved him. She wanted to hold him in her hands and feel his soft, furry body. He was breathing so fast now, it wouldn't be long. She returned him to his plastic tower, washed her hands, and crawled under her covers. Clifford curled up beside her.

"I'm so tired, boy," she said. "But I'm not sure I can fall asleep."

She stroked his fur for a while, and he licked her hand, and eventually, she must have drifted off. Not long after, she heard a noise, opened her eyes, and saw Than standing over her bed.

Chapter Eight: Death Comes

Therese stared at him, astonished. She barely noticed the rain falling outside her window. Thump, thump, thump. Was it rain? Or was it the pounding of her heart?

Than looked down at her and smiled. It was a sober smile. It wasn't unfriendly, but it lacked enthusiasm and was sad. He was wearing his loose-fitting trousers and open white shirt and brown leather sandals. His dark hair hadn't grown an inch since she had last seen him and just reached his bright blue eyes.

"Am I dreaming?" She tried to push off into the air but remained solidly on the bed.

"No," he replied.

"Figment!" she nearly shouted. "I command you to show yourself!"

Than stood over her. He hadn't disappeared. "It's me, Therese."

Her mouth dropped open and she jumped to her knees. She twisted the front of her t-shirt in both hands, like she was wringing out a wet rag. She hardly realized what she was doing. In her dreams, she always knew what to do; but now that she was actually looking upon the real Than, she felt speechless and paralyzed.

Clifford stood from where he had been lying beside her and wagged his tail. He gave a playful bark, which brought Therese back to her senses.

"Hi, Clifford," Than said.

"You've come for me, then? Finally? After all these months?" The initial shock wore off. She threw her arms around his neck and immediately felt the cold creeping through her body, the air harder to breathe. But she held him and felt a sense of relief. She wouldn't have to risk her life with Vicki after all.

He gave her one quick kiss and then pushed her back down onto the bed. "I came for Puffy, not for you, Therese. Please stay back so I don't kill you."

As she fell back, she heard his words, took them in, felt their sting. Frustration and disappointment turned into anger. "You're never coming for me, are you? You won't come till I'm dead!"

He frowned. "I've been busy. It's dangerous for you to be close to me while I'm the guide for the dead. I thought you understood." He moved to Puffy's cage.

"If Puffy hadn't died..." she couldn't complete the thought out loud. She felt dizzy and breathless. He hadn't come for her. He was just doing his job. Did he care for her at all? Had he ever loved her? She studied him in profile as he dipped his hand through Puffy's plastic tower and pulled out an orb of light in Puffy's image. Puffy's body remained in the tower curled up in the bedding.

"It's okay, Puffy," he said to the hamster. "I'm here to guide you." Then to Therese, he said, "I didn't have to wake you up and show myself to you. I thought you'd be glad to see me. I guess it was a mistake."

"You're a god, for heaven's sake! If you really loved me, you'd find a way to be with me." She saw the pain in his face, and for a split moment regretted her words. Then he turned from her with Puffy in his hand, and the anger moved swiftly over her again. "Answer me, Than! How much longer?"

The rain fell more heavily and a crash of thunder roared in the distance. The late afternoon thunder showers had come.

"I don't know. Be patient. I need to go before you get too weak, before I kill you." He backed away.

She leapt from the bed and wrapped her arms around him again, desperate and trembling, and now, gasping for air. She held onto his neck and pressed her cheek against his warm, bare chest. Not with her gaping, blue lips, but in prayer, she said, "I'm sorry. I didn't mean to yell. I miss you so much." Her stomach felt like she was going to be sick. The air felt thick, her efforts at breathing stifled, but she held on. It felt so good to be against him, to feel his body with her own. It felt so wonderful to see him, to squeeze his hand, run fingers through his hair, to know he was real. There were a thousand things she had wanted to ask, but her head was spinning. She couldn't think of what she had wanted to say, and she was frustrated, having longed for this moment for months. Not wanting the moment to end, she clung to him, tried to look into his eyes, and, as he forcefully pried her blue fingers from his neck, fell back into unconsciousness.

When she came to, Than was gone and Puffy had stopped breathing.

She replayed the few minutes Than had been in her room in slow motion. She at first felt the joy of seeing him and the pleasure of being in his presence. Her body felt aroused as she recalled the feel of him against her, her fingers in his hair. But the pleasure turned to pain, and the pain to anger.

She touched Puffy's stiff body without moving him from his plastic tower. Tears rushed from her eyes. "Say hi to Mom and Dad for me." She decided at that moment she hated Than, the god of the dead, and she wished she had never met him. But she would tell him to his face. She would take the NDE drug with Vicki next weekend, she would march to the gates of hell, and she would tell the son of a you-know-what to his face that she never wanted to see him again. Even when she died, she wanted someone else to come for her!

How hard could it be for a god to give her a better indication of what he was doing to try and get her back? Had he worked out a new agreement with his father? Or had he been doing his job with no time for anything but the dead?

Than had said Therese would be unhappy spending eternity in the Underworld. Maybe he hoped she would gradually forget about him. Maybe he was staying away from her because he thought it was best for her.

Then why had he showed himself to her today? Had it been a moment of weakness?

The concept of time was different to the gods, so maybe to Than, ten months was like a snap of the fingers. But hadn't he heard all her desperate prayers? If he had a heart, he'd tell her something more than "I've been busy. Be patient."

She moved to her bed and wept, and after a few moments, Carol knocked at her door.

"Are you okay in there? Can I come in?" Carol opened the door.

"Puffy died," Therese said, sobbing.

"Oh, sweetheart, I'm so sorry." Carol leaned over and gave Therese a hug. The smell of Haiku perfume and Jergen's lotion washed over Therese. It was the same smell of her mother. Carol sat on the bed beside her, and for a moment, Therese thought it was her mother. She almost said, "Mom." Almost. She blinked.

"I know you were expecting this," Carol said, "but even then, it's never easy. Maybe you should stay home tonight."

Therese nodded, still sobbing, all the forces of grief sweeping over her. She felt she might drown even though the rain outside had finally stopped.

"You want me to call the Holts?"

Therese nodded again and then buried her face in her pillow.

Carol kissed the back of Therese's head and closed the door behind her as she left the room.

Therese lay there thinking how much she hated Than. She refused to pray her thoughts to him. She would keep them to herself until she could seek him out and tell him to his face what she thought of him. She knew she was the only one who ever prayed to him in a loving way. He had told her so himself. Except for the desperate pleas of those near death, or from the loved ones beside the deathbed, begging him to change a course he could not change, she was the only voice he heard. Hers was the cheer in his life, he had said. Well, forget that. If he couldn't give her a better explanation, he could feel the same silence she had been feeling on her end.

She finally understood the warning Artemis and Athena had given her about women who loved immortal men and understood why Daphne, a nymph, ran from Apollo and begged her river-father to turn her into a tree.

She tried to recall why she ever thought she loved him and remembered his face turned up to the rain with pleasure. Later he had put his arm around her and comforted her after Dumbo's fatal accident. His face lit up whenever he looked upon the sunset, and his eyes brightened when he moved through the cool water of the lake. A giggle escaped from her throat when she recalled teaching him to waltz, but she quickly sobered at the memory of how he had held her on the dance floor of the Wildhorse Saloon and had touched her like he had never touched a human being. He had relished her lips as much as she had relished his.

She thought of the three sunsets they had visited in one day. The way he had defended her on Mount Olympus. The care he took when he helped her sort through her parents' things.

And he had begged Aphrodite to save Clifford's life because he knew Therese couldn't take another death.

But he had said he would come back for her, and almost a year had passed since he made that promise. Tonight he said he'd been busy. He'd been too busy for her. He hadn't even come to see her. He was only doing his job. Maybe he'd changed his mind. He didn't love her after all.

She hated him. And she couldn't wait to tell him.

She hugged her pillow. If only she had killed McAdams. She'd be with Than now and forever. Why was she blaming him? She was the one who had failed.

But she was only a human. He was a god, for crying out loud. He said he'd come for her and he hadn't. Would she be an old maid before he finally found time in his busy schedule for her?

Therese wasn't sure how much time had passed when another knock came at her door.

"Therese, it's me, Jen. I'm coming in."

Therese didn't get up from the bed. Jen came over and hugged her just as Carol had done. Too much Oscar de la Renta made Therese cough. She noticed Vicki hovering in the doorway as though she was afraid to get too close. Maybe she thought she couldn't encroach on Jen's territory. Jen sat on the bed.

"I'm sorry about Puffy," Jen said.

"Me, too," Vicki said from the doorway.

"Thanks guys. I'm sorry I'm canceling out on you tonight. I hope you understand."

Jen put a hand on each of Therese's shoulders and squared herself to her friend, leaning over her. Therese noticed how pretty Jen looked in makeup, something Jen rarely wore and really didn't need. Her blonde hair fell forward around her face and smelled of hairspray, but the hair itself wasn't stiff. Her pale blue blouse, however, was stiff and wrinkle-free and had probably been starched and ironed. A rhinestone belt buckle showed off her thin waistline. "But lying in bed all evening is the last thing you should do. All this grief is going to build up and eat you alive. I know you, Therese Mills, and you're not just crying over Puffy. I mean, I know you're hurt. I know you loved him. But you're thinking of your parents, too, and probably Dumbo. Am I right?"

The tears gushed from Therese's eyes. Her friend knew her well. "Than...called." Therese hated the lie, but the truth was unbelievable.

Jen stood upright, nearly falling back. "Oh my God! What did he say?"

Therese fought the sobs. "He said he's been busy. He wants me to be patient."

"That jerk!" Jen shouted. Carol and Richard might have heard.

"I hate him, Jen. I hate him so bad. I feel sick!" Therese climbed from her bed and ran to her bathroom where she threw up in the commode.

Jen followed her in and patted Therese, bent over the bowl as she kneeled on the floor, coughing. Jen got her a clean towel from the cabinet. "I hate him, too," Jen said. "And I tell you what. The best thing you can do is go out tonight and dance your butt off with as many guys as you can. Help yourself forget about him. If he calls again, you can tell him *you're* busy, and you won't be lying!"

The idea didn't sound too bad. "I don't know."

"Matthew's out in the truck and Todd and Ray are in Todd's truck behind us. Todd wanted to follow Matthew. And Bobby will be there, too. You'll have plenty of dance partners to keep your mind off of you know who. And Pete's band won't be playing all night. They're one group of a handful. Pete'll want to dance with you, too. Come on, what do you say?"

Vicki now hovered in the doorway of the bathroom. For the first time, Therese noticed how pretty she looked with her hair pulled away from her face instead of scraggily falling into it. Her brown eyes had been outlined with make up, and her pale cheeks had spots of color. She wore a summer dress and sandals—which would be hard to dance in on the concrete floor at the Pagosa Springs Fairgrounds, but her slight figure and toothpick legs were softened by them. "I think you should go for it. I agree with Jen."

"But I haven't even showered."

Jen helped Therese to her feet. "That's alright. We'll wait for you downstairs. I'll tell the guys to come in. I'll go make some Crystal Light lemonade and some of that spray cheese on crackers. I saw it all out on the counter on the way up. We'll be fine."

Jen and Vicki left the room.

As Therese showered and the warm water fell over her, she caught herself starting to talk to Than. She had been praying to him for ten long months, and it had become a habit. She wasn't always aware she was doing it. He had become her invisible best friend, and cutting off communication with him would be harder than she had at first thought. So maybe she would channel her thoughts to another god. She decided Poseidon might not be the best pick, because she still suspected he might have had something to do with that morning's earthquake. And although she really liked Artemis, the goddess of wild things hadn't been too happy with her at their last encounter. Artemis thought Therese was stupid for loving Than. Athena had said the same last summer. Well, maybe both goddesses would be glad to hear Therese's plan of action. But what if Therese changed her mind? What if she eventually decided she didn't hate Than? Would Artemis and Athena be tolerant of her indecision? What if the goddesses turned on Than?

Now Aphrodite, the goddess of love, understood love's ups and downs, but Aphrodite might not like Therese's plan of going to the Underworld and telling Than off. Aphrodite might try to talk her out of it.

58

Therese didn't want to risk that. She was dead bent on telling off Than to his face.

Persephone and Demeter wouldn't do, either. They were Than's mother and grandmother. Therese couldn't expect them to have an unbiased stance. They'd probably sympathize with Than and thwart Therese's efforts.

Of course Ares was out of the question. The god of war had been behind her parents' death. He wanted to prevent her mother from finding the cure to the mutated Anthrax C. He wanted foreign coups to have a useful store of the mutated Anthrax so a new balance of power could come into the world. Ares wanted to see America fall. Plus, he hated Therese and would take any opportunity to bring her down. He was against her becoming a god because he knew he could never count on her support.

Zeus was just out of her league. She was scared to death of him. Hades, too. Besides, Hades clearly showed his disdain for her when she refused to kill McAdams. And Than's sisters, the Furies, were intimidating to say the least. She couldn't shrug off their description of the way they beat information out of their suspects: blood dripped from their eyes, snakes crawled through their hair, and piercing screams came from their throats. No, Therese didn't think she'd pray to them.

She didn't really know Hestia, Hera, Apollo, or Hephaestus. But Hermes! The messenger of the gods had once been her friend.

Therese rinsed the shampoo from her hair and embraced this new idea of Hermes. He had liked Therese. They played their instruments together and shared laughs together and he had been supportive on Mount Olympus. He had had his share of love affairs and children and so could understand Therese's heartbreak. And yet, Therese had the sense he wouldn't let her hatred of Than ruin his own relationship with the god of the dead. Hermes it was.

59

She turned off the shower and dried off, and as she put on her blue jeans and green cotton blouse, she attempted her first prayer to him: "Hermes, do you remember me? It's Therese. I hope you don't mind if I talk to you. Thanatos has broken my heart."

She threw on a little makeup and blow-dried her hair. That was enough for now. She would wait and tell Hermes her plans later. Tonight, she was going to have fun and forget all about Than. Around her neck was Athena's locket reminding her that *the most common way people give up their power is by believing they have none.*

Chapter Nine: The Maenads

"Go with food," Demeter had said, "and a belly full of wine." Than's grandmother had no other words of wisdom, tricks, or ideas to help him get on Dionysus's good side except to go into the forest of Mount Kithairon at night emboldened with alcohol and offering food. If he hesitated and showed the slightest insecurity, he would be ripped to pieces.

"They may rip you to pieces anyway," she had said.

So here he was, only yards away from where the god and his followers were said to be, and his confidence waned. He had a bag of food slung over his shoulder—fruits and bread Demeter had given him—but he hadn't taken his grandmother's advice concerning the wine. He wanted to be in control of his actions. He could be merry and bold without alcohol—at least, he hoped he could as he crept through the woods.

Much of the mountain was bare and rocky, but here, in a smattering of thick pines, he could see a campfire in the distance and a hazy line of smoke rising into the night sky. Laughter and singing made the group seem less daunting, but a sudden demonic shriek chilled him and made him hesitate again. Then an idea came to him, hard and fast like a thunderbolt: his sisters. The Furies. Their presence might help his cause. He hadn't asked for help because he didn't want his father to get wind of his plans and try to stop him, but now that he was irrevocably in the middle of them, he disintegrated and dispatched to seek his sisters out. Meanwhile, he slowly stole through the woods, hoping to catch a glimpse of the maenads before they noticed him.

Seeing Therese so angry and hurt this afternoon when he went for the hamster had added a greater sense of urgency to Than's already urgent mission. If his presence wasn't lethal to her, he would have stayed to give a report on his progress, but that was impossible. Hell, he would have swept her in his arms and caressed her face with his lips. He would have...oh, he moaned as he picked through the branches. If she really loved him and had faith in him, she'd wait. Her lot was to wait. His was far worse. His foot cracked a twig and caught the attention of a woman standing ten feet away, on the outskirts of the group.

She looked back at him suspiciously. Her curly brown hair was knotted on her head and ringed with ivy. She wore animal skins around her breasts and hips, but her shoulders and legs were bare, and she held a thyrsus—a staff tipped with a pinecone. "What's this?" She spoke softly, to herself. No one else in the group seemed to notice.

"I bring gifts," he said, holding out an orange. "I've come to celebrate, if you'll have me."

His heart raced as he awaited her reply. She narrowed her eyes and took a step closer. "Is it a real orange? They're my favorite, you know."

He tossed it to her. "It's yours. From Demeter, my grandmother."

The woman caught the orange, tore off the peel in less than five seconds, and put the meat to her nose. She smiled and savagely devoured the fruit. She turned to Than with juice dripping down her chin. "Who are you?"

"Someone who has finally found true love." It sounded trite, but it was true, and he thought these women, who danced and loved and drank, would appreciate it. He knew if he revealed himself, he'd disgust her. No one wants Death. "May I join the party?"

At that moment, another woman turned and noticed him. Her curly black hair flowed around her face, which was stained red with blood

62

or wine, Than didn't know which. She held a chalice in one hand and a thyrsus in the other. A panther skin hung over her shoulder, its head still intact at her breast. "Who's this?"

"He says he's found true love," the first maenad said to the other. "For a moment, I thought he meant me."

"We're about to dance," she said. "The flutes and lyres are warmed up. We can't wait for introductions." The woman turned her back to him and began to move her body in a jerky, frenzied movement, not too unlike what Than had seen with epileptics as they fell to their deaths.

The first maenad took his hand and tugged him along the perimeter of the other raving dancers. What began as a soft tap-tap of the drums exploded into a booming, pounding thrash. Than did his best to mimic the movements of the others, feeling foolish but desperate to win their approval. The maenad on the end of his arm shrieked with joy and jerked around like a raving lunatic. Soon he felt himself surrounded by the throng of moving bodies bumping against him. The ecstatic women in the crowd seemed oblivious to his presence and to each other, as though lost in a trance, each singing her own song. The chaos and confusion were overwhelming, making it difficult for Than to feign joy.

This difficulty increased when the maenads fell upon a snake someone had thrown into the dancers. He watched with disgust as they tore the creature to pieces and stuffed chunks of it into their mouths. He disintegrated to escort the snake's soul. Next came a rabbit, flung through the air by someone he could not see and caught in the hands of the mass of women, ripping and tearing the terrified, struggling creature. He disintegrated again. The bodies soon made way for two maenads pulling a thrashing buck by the horns into the center. Its limbs and head were ripped from its body and devoured by the dancers. Another disintegration. Than fragmented constantly, multiple times per second, so often did the living die. A second group fell on the remaining lump of carcass quivering in the grass until it was eaten up, blood dripping down chins.

"Now we are one with nature," one of them said in a bold voice. "Their souls belong to us."

Than decided now would not be a good time to correct her. Their souls had gone on. Instead, he opened his sack and tossed oranges and apples to the crowd. The fruit was gladly received and consumed as savagely as the animals. A ring of dancers formed around Than. They touched his arms and mussed his hair, smiling at him seductively. Then one maenad circled her arms around his waist and kissed him on the lips. As suddenly as she had come to him, she pulled away, screaming.

"Death!" she cried. "Death is among us!"

The joyful faces turned to panic and terror. Than wasn't sure why. They were immortal. He had suspected they wouldn't be too keen to see him if they knew his identity, but he never thought they'd fear him.

"Death is among us!" another shrieked.

At first the maenads scattered from him, leaving him alone in the center of their ring. Then someone yelled, "Kill him! Kill Death, so we can live forever!"

Before Than could say anything, the raving women rushed at him and grabbed a hold of his arms.

"Wait!" He struggled against them, trying not to hurt them as he flung them from his side. "Get back! Get back! Back, I say!"

A maenad grasped his thumb and tore it from his hand, sending shards of pain, deep and intense, through his arm and head. "Ahhh!" He held the hurt hand in the other and once again shouted, "Back!" as he now elbowed the women more forcefully than he dared to before, his blood spurting onto their dresses and skin.

Where were his sisters? He'd been hunting for them in Tartarus and all over the globe. He didn't dare ask his father where they were;

64

Hades would want to know why. Than prayed out to them again and again. "Mount Kithairon! I need you at Mount Kithairon!"

To the maenads, he shouted, "Get back and listen to me! I haven't come to take anyone! I've come to see Dionysus!" His hand throbbed. He spotted the woman with his thumb and he charged at her and took it back, but at the sound of their lord's name, the maenads stopped attacking him. He stood, bewildered by their silence and stillness, searching their faces. Then a youthful god about his own age strolled to the center of the ring to face him. A group of satyrs hovered behind him. His hair was golden, like Hip's, but long and braided in two ropes at the back of his head. He wore nothing but a strap of leather at his loins.

"What does Death want with me?"

"A favor," Than replied.

Dionysus lifted his head and laughed, and the maenads and satyrs did the same.

Than spotted Alecto materialize above him, but he warned her off. "Tell the others I don't need them," he prayed silently to her. "And please, say nothing of this to our father."

She vanished, but he sensed her presence. Dionysus did, too.

"What will you do for me in return, Thanatos?"

"Anything that is within my power." He felt himself losing blood at the wound where his thumb should be. He was in agony, but did well to hide it.

Dionysus's merry smile faded and he jutted his chin. "Indeed. Leave us, maenads. Follow the satyrs up the mountain."

The satyrs played a melody on their wooden flutes and led a parade of women further up the mountain. Once they were gone, Than carefully molded his thumb back to his hand and healed it, asking, "Why do they fear me when they're immortal?" The pain continued, but the thumb was back, and though it hurt, he could move it a little. How long it would be before he had full strength in it, he didn't know. He'd never, in his ancient life, sustained an injury such as this. He could only imagine the pain of enduring his entire body ripped this way.

"Only the wine keeps them so. Without me and the fruit of my vines, they would die."

"Tell them I'm your servant."

"There *is* something I want."

Chapter Ten: The Festival

Therese was surprised by the happiness she felt when she went downstairs to the gallery of friends awaiting her. She hadn't seen Todd and Ray since school let out four weeks ago, and they always managed to lift her spirits.

Ray, a chubby, but tall, Native American with dark eyes and short thick black hair, started things off, as usual. He wore his signature look: an open plaid shirt with a t-shirt underneath, jeans, and sneakers. Unlike Todd, he refused to dress like a cowboy since he wasn't actually a cowboy, and Todd, who also wasn't one, but who looked like one with his tall, wiry frame and Wrangler jeans and boots, was the butt of a lot of Ray's jokes: "You know what the urban cowboy would say…" and so forth. Now, Ray stood up and asked, "Why does it always take girls so long? I mean, what do they do, shave their legs by plucking one hair at a time? Or maybe there's some kind of good luck ritual they have to go through before they even get started."

Jen gave Ray a look that said "Not tonight," but Therese actually laughed.

"You're on to us," Therese said, "on both counts."

The rest of the group stood now, too, and Todd said, "Come see what I've done to my truck." It was a fifty-seven Chevy painted bright yellow and mounted high on a lift kit. They all said goodnight to Carol and Richard and headed outside.

Matthew linked his hand into Jen's as they walked down the steps to the gravelly drive, and Therese felt a stab of pain pierce her chest. She blinked and pushed the pain away, telling herself tonight would be a good time with good friends and nothing else mattered.

"Oh, hold on. I forgot something." Therese ran back inside, up the stairs to her room and into her desk drawer. She had promised to give

Vicki the money for the NDE drugs, and she didn't want anything holding up their plans. She ran back out just as the group gathered around Todd's truck. "Okay. So what's new?"

"Check out my chrome. I was so excited when I found this authentic fifty-seven grill. Now my truck matches. Cool, huh?"

"Very cool," Therese said. "It looks so shiny and new. You wouldn't know it was an antique." She enjoyed making a big deal over Todd's truck because she knew how important it was to him. She would have liked to ride with him and Ray, but she knew Vicki would feel like a third wheel riding in Matthew's truck, which had an extended cab, and the two girls couldn't fit in Todd's, which did not. So Therese oooed and awed and then climbed into the backseat of Matthew's truck beside Vicki.

Once they were on the road, Therese silently passed the one hundred dollars over to Vicki, who nodded, folded the bills, and tucked them into her purse.

The Pagosa Springs Fairgrounds were a happening place by the time the two vehicles arrived. They had to drive up and down a dusty dirt parking lot for over fifteen minutes looking for a place to park. They each finally found one a couple of hundred yards away from the entrance. Therese's boots were covered in white dust by the time they paid their cover and entered the grounds.

Carnival rides and game and food booths were scattered across the grassy field that was surrounded by mountains still visible in the summer evening. As the group walked through the lane between the booths, they recognized people they knew and occasionally stopped to talk. Then they continued their way to the dance area where they looked forward to watching Pete's band perform.

Someone came up from behind Therese, tucked his hands beneath her armpits, and lifted her in the air, spinning her around and making her laugh. She could tell before he put her down that she was in Pete's hands. She turned to face him.

"When's your band onstage?"

"About eight." He led the group to a table where the rest of the Holts were already sitting, except for Bobby, who was dancing the two-step on the concrete dance floor with some girl Therese didn't know. "Ready?"

Pete smelled and felt good as he led Therese to the dance floor and took her in his arms. His white cowboy hat brought out the glow in his tanned face and sparkling blue eyes. His nose was sprinkled with a few summer freckles, and when he smiled, his teeth were pearl white. His shoulders were broad and well defined in the starched denim shirt unbuttoned at the very top. His jeans were tight, hugging his backside in a flattering way. Therese wanted to reach out and touch it. She was surprised by how good she felt in his arms, how much she liked him, and now that she was finally giving up on Than, Pete had her undivided attention.

He was a master at dancing—such a good lead that she hardly had to think at all. He twirled her around and past the other dancers in show-off fashion. She squealed a couple of times when he lifted her over his head.

And his voice was as smooth as her father's red wine, which he let her taste when she turned thirteen. She loved to listen to Pete sing the lyrics he knew; and when he didn't know the words to a song, he hummed softly in her ear, sending tingles down her neck and back.

When Todd wanted to cut in after several songs, Pete complained. "I'll have to go on stage soon and you can have her then."

Todd reluctantly backed off the floor and settled for Vicki.

Therese noticed Vicki didn't know how to dance, but Todd was patient with her and took things slow. He kept to a very basic step, talking her through the moves.

The salty taste of sweat made Therese lick her lips. Beads of sweat were pouring down her face and Pete's. They had danced at least a dozen songs—a couple of polkas and swings, several Texas Two Steps, and one slow waltz that had her closing her eyes and imagining a life with Pete. Now Pete asked if she wanted something to drink.

"I need a break before I go on stage," he said.

"A diet coke sounds good."

He walked her to one of the booths on the side of the dance area. "Diet? Why do you drink diet? You sure don't need to watch your weight."

"I just like the taste better. Regular coke tastes too sweet to me."

He gave her a quick and spontaneous peck on the lips. Then with a devilish smile, he asked, "Do I taste too sweet to you?"

She felt the heat rush to her face. "No, definitely not, Peter Holt," was all she could think to say as she turned away toward the booth.

They got in line behind four or five others. "Jen texted me about your hamster. I'm sorry you lost him, but I'm glad you decided to come tonight. My night wouldn't have been the same."

"I'm glad I came, too. You're such a great dancer. I'm having fun."

He blushed and kissed her again with a quick peck on the cheek, which made her blush, again, too. Then it was time for him to get their drinks. He bought himself a Sprite.

"I can pay for my pop," Therese said, but he wouldn't let her. "Then I'll get the next round."

They caught up with the others at the Holts' table when Pete suddenly said, "We gotta ride the octopus."

70

Therese gave him a doubtful look.

"Come on. It's my favorite ride, and I have a little more time before I go on."

Jen joined in. "Let's all go. What do you think, Matthew?"

"I'm in," Ray said before Matthew replied.

So a whole group of them ran off to get some tickets and get in line for the octopus.

On the ride, Therese sat against Pete, who had his arm around her, as one of the black tentacles whipped them around in the air. She shouted, delirious, not having laughed this hard in a long, long time. Todd and Vicki were in another car, Jen and Matthew in another, and Ray rode alone, with his arms up in the air. When the ride scooped down, Therese buried her face in Pete's chest.

"Oh my God!" she said, her stomach lurching.

Not long after, Pete left her standing near the table by the Holts talking to Ray as they watched Todd and Vicki, Matthew and Jen, and Bobby and his new partner dance to some transitional, pre-recorded music while Pete's band set up. When Pete's smooth voice finally rang out across the Fairgrounds, his crystal eyes and gorgeous smile directed at Therese, she felt surprisingly content. She felt as though he was singing exclusively for her, and she really didn't mind the occasional eyes in the audience who would seek out the object of the singer's attention. For the rest of the evening, Todd and Bobby danced with her, but not without Pete getting in his winks and waves to her. After Pete's band finished its one hour performance and put away the equipment, Pete came back to reclaim her for the evening.

Therese was dizzy with excitement. Pete had not been shy about showing his feelings for her, and she was overwhelmed. But it was a good feeling. She liked the feeling. She had encouraged Pete tonight more than she had all year, and it felt so, so good. By the time the group was ready

71

to go, Pete had convinced Therese to ride back with him. Todd offered to take Vicki home, which took pressure off of her: she didn't have to worry about Vicki feeling like a third wheel with Matthew and Jen.

Pete helped her in on the passenger side, and then went around to the other. When she started to strap herself in near the door, he objected and pulled her over to the middle of the bench seat beside him. She laughed and was delighted by his strength and persistence. He put his hand on her thigh. She covered his hand with hers.

They talked about school—about band and her classes. Then he asked about her plans after high school. She didn't know. Probably college, but not Fort Lewis. It reminded her too much of her mom.

He asked how she was doing with her parents' death, and it felt good to talk about it honestly with someone.

"I still sometimes act a little loony," she said. "I'll be in the mall or at the movies, and I'll see someone with my mom's red hair or my dad's build, and I'll almost call out to them. I guess I still can't accept that they're really gone."

"That's understandable." He squeezed her hand.

She asked if he planned to stay working at the Holt Ranch.

"I'm really happy right now. I work with the horses, get to be around my family, and get to play a few gigs with my band here and there. I feel like I've got everything I want right here. I don't plan to go anywhere." He gave her a wink.

"How's it going with your dad home? Jen doesn't talk about it. I noticed both your parents were drinking pop tonight."

He sighed. "I don't know. I think my dad might be drinking again. Ever since that one night, I guess once you fall off the wagon it's hard to get back on again. It's another reason for me not to go anywhere."

"What makes you think he's drinking again?"

"Well, don't say anything to Jen."

72

"No, of course not."

"The other day the toilet in our main bathroom wouldn't flush, so I took off the lid of the tank. Inside I found a half-empty bottle of rum. It was a big bottle, leaning in the corner of the tank."

"That's kind of weird. What did you do?"

"I thought about confronting him. I mean, there was a slight chance he had left it there from before."

"Very slight, I would think."

"We hadn't looked in that tank in forever."

"Yeah, you could be right."

"But then I decided to pour it out in the grass and throw the bottle away. If he had put it there recently, it would still send a message someone's on to him."

"But wouldn't he just find better hiding places?"

He shrugged. "I guess I should confront him." He gave her a glance and she nodded.

"I think so. It's the only way to get closure." She was thinking of her own plans to confront Than.

He asked if she would be coming over to groom Stormy tomorrow.

"He's so cute. He'll help me keep my mind off of my hamster."

As they reached Lemon Dam, Pete turned off onto another country road and pulled over. Therese wanted to ask what he was doing, but she already knew.

"There's something I want to tell you, Therese."

She couldn't look at him. She had been so happy to be with him, had felt awesome in his arms, and had been filled with a sincere joy all evening; but now as he was about to say words she already knew, her heart felt gripped with pain and fear. Something wasn't right. Something wasn't right about this at all.

73

Maybe it was that she hadn't yet told off Than. Maybe she needed to get her feelings off her chest and tell Than where he could go—he was already in hell, anyway—before she could move forward with Pete. Determined that this was the cause of the uneasy feeling, she interrupted Pete and said, "Wait."

Before she could say more, he leaned in and touched his lips to hers. This was no quick peck. His mouth felt warm and good, and something eased up in her chest as she sighed. He put his arms around her and pressed her close to him. His hard chest and strong arms made her feel like she was melting. His kisses moved around her mouth, across her chin, down her neck, toward her throat.

"Wait," she said again, pulling back.

"I'm sorry."

"There's something I have to do," she said. "I haven't officially broken things off with Than. But this weekend, I'm going to do it. I'm going to tell him I don't want to see him again. Once I do that, I'll feel better about this, with you. You know?"

Pete slowly nodded and leaned back. The disappointment was obvious in his face. "I didn't realize you two were still a couple."

"We really haven't been much of one. I just want to be sure. I need closure."

"I understand."

He drove her home, and on the way, he kept both hands on the wheel. They rode in silence, barely touching. When they reached her house she said, "I had a really great time tonight. Thanks for bringing me home."

"My pleasure." He didn't offer her a goodnight kiss, but he gave her a wink to let her know he understood.

She slid from the bench seat and made her way toward her house, shaking like a leaf. She hoped she knew what she was doing.

74

"Help me, Hermes," she whispered as she lay in bed next to her dog. "Thanatos has broken my heart. I plan to say goodbye to him forever. I need to go on, right? Tell me what to do."

She fell asleep saying her prayers.

Chapter Eleven: Ariadne

Than appeared before the palace ruins of Knossos on the island of Crete under which the ancient labyrinth of the Minotaur lay mostly intact. He'd been here many times to collect the souls of the beast's victims. He had waited till dark so as not to draw attention from tourists as he scoured the ruins for the entrance and its guardian, the beautiful Ariadne and wife of Dionysus. The god of wine agreed to help Than if he could convince Ariadne to return to Mount Kithairon and his side.

No expert when it came to matters of the heart, Than wasn't sure he could succeed, but he had to try. Already, Therese's prayers had become less frequent, and he feared he would lose her heart altogether. In fact, he couldn't recall hearing her lovely voice since he saw her last at Puffy's departure. Her voice had been like food to him, and now he was starving.

A subtle glow appeared beneath a fallen pillar. He immediately sensed another godly presence. He traveled through the rock into a cavern, and backed against the wall was a lovely raven-haired goddess he knew must be Ariadne.

"Are you here for a victim of the Minotaur?"

"No."

"Then why?"

"As a favor to Dionysus."

She dropped her eyes and linked her fingers together. "He wouldn't come himself?"

"Too many depend on him. The maenads would die, and they're needed to enforce the oaths."

"He hasn't the power of disintegration afforded to you and your brother."

"Correct. Few of us can be in many places at once."

She looked up at him again. "I did not know you were beautiful. I've seen your brother, and knew of his beauty, but not of yours."

Than blushed. "Most people avoid me because of my job."

She stepped closer to him, her eyes taking him in and making him uneasy. "Few know I was married to Dionysus before I left him for Theseus. I couldn't help myself. Dionysus is beautiful. But Theseus was courageous and honorable. Dionysus cares little for honor."

"It's not honorable to steal away with another man's wife."

"Theseus was unaware."

"But you weren't. You helped him kill the Minotaur and then ran away with him." This was not the way to win her over, he thought. "You must have had your reasons."

"Dionysus is always surrounded by women."

"But none more beautiful than you. Nor more temperate." Of course, that was true of any woman. The maenads weren't hard to beat in temperance.

"What does he want?"

"You by his side. He wants to leave the past in the past. Theseus is in the Underworld now, barely aware of his own history. You have a long life, an immortal one. You could find happiness at Mount Kithairon. Here you're alone."

"You forget the Minotaur, who at no fault of his own, has been imprisoned in this labyrinth. He can't help what his parents did and what he is as a result. Why should he be made to suffer alone, while Dionysus and I drink wine and dance in the woods of Mount Kithairon?"

"You love the Minotaur?"

"I betrayed him once, as you said. I pity him."

"More than you love your husband?"

She stepped closer to Than and searched his eyes, her mouth open and moist. He thought she would kiss him. He stepped back.

"Maybe," she said. "I don't know."

"Go back with me to Mount Kithairon and discover the depth of your love for Dionysus. You can always leave again."

"Why do you care what I do?"

"I love someone."

She stepped closer, her eyes inches from him. "Who?"

"A mortal. I want to make her a god and need your husband's help. He will only consent if you return to his side." Than went down on his knees. "So I beg you, beautiful Ariadne, guardian of the labyrinth. Maybe you could do as my mother does and spend half your time down here and the other half in the woods of Mount Kithairon."

She went down on her knees before him so her eyes were level with his mouth. "Perhaps if you lie with me, I'll do you this favor."

Than swallowed hard, his throat suddenly dry. No one had ever come on to him like this in the history of his existence. It felt good. Tempting. It occurred to him that if things didn't go right with Therese— no, there could be no one else. Just thinking otherwise broke his heart. "Who wouldn't be flattered by such a proposition? But my heart belongs to another, and I won't betray her. I'll do anything else. Name it."

Ariadne climbed to her feet, her eyes narrowed and her lips pursed. "Go down into the labyrinth then and find your way out before the Minotaur rips your heart out and devours it, and only then will I go with you to Mount Kithairon."

Chapter Twelve: The NDE Drug

Therese woke up late Sunday morning, unable to recall her dream. She took Clifford out, fed and watered him and Jewels, and then noticed Puffy's body was not in his cage. She ran downstairs again.

"Where's Puffy?"

Richard and Carol had already eaten, but a plate of pancakes waited for her.

"He's right here." Carol pointed to a floral box on the counter by the kitchen sink. "A scented candle came in that box, and it still smells really nice. I put Puffy in there last night so, so you wouldn't have to. I would have cleaned his cage and put it away, but I wasn't sure whether you wanted me to or not."

"Thanks," Therese said. "I want to do it myself."

"I dug a hole," Richard said from the sofa across the room. "Out by one of the elms. We could bury him there, if you'd like."

Therese smiled, her eyes welling, just a little bit. "That would be nice. I'll go get dressed."

She threw on some jeans and a t-shirt and came back down.

The three of them went outside in the back of the house beneath one of two giant elm trees and committed Puffy to the earth. "Ashes to ashes, dust to dust," Therese murmured. Her dad had bought her the hamster four years ago. Puffy's death was one more thing separating her from her parents. She wiped her tears with the back of her hand as her throat constricted, and she felt inexplicably angry at Richard and Carol.

Richard covered the hole up with dirt while Therese and Carol watched on. Then he patted the earth down, leaned the shovel against the tree, and said, "There we go."

The three walked back into the house.

"Did you have fun last night?" Carol asked. She went back to doing something on her laptop.

Therese started on her pancakes. "Yeah, I had fun. We all did."

As she ate her breakfast at the countertop, Therese told her aunt and uncle she was headed over to the Holts to groom Stormy, and Clifford would be going along, too, if that was okay.

With their blessing, she and Clifford walked down the three-quarter-mile path to Jen's house along the dirt road separating the mountain homes from Lemon Reservoir. Clifford stopped to pee on nearly every tree, so Therese had to keep saying, "Come on, boy."

She felt a little nervous about seeing Pete today.

But Pete was as friendly as always and immediately put her at ease. The whole family was already out with the horses. They didn't offer trail rides on Sundays, so they looked forward to finishing up their chores and taking the afternoon off. Jen asked Therese if she wanted to go shopping with her.

"Maybe. What are you shopping for?"

"Nothing. I just want to look at dresses, to get some ideas for prom."

Therese rolled her eyes. "I guess I can go with you, but you do realize prom's like, light-years away from now?"

Jen laughed. "I guess I'm excited, you know?"

Therese stroked Stormy with a soft towel as Jen worked on Sassy. She couldn't believe how big he was getting. He nuzzled her hand.

The whole week went that way. Carol and Richard were supportive, Pete was easy to talk to, Jen asked her to do things with her, and Therese felt surprisingly okay with Puffy's death. She cleaned and put away the cage. She wasn't ready for a new hamster, but she stored the cage in the basement just in case she felt differently one day.

Thursday, Vicki called to say she had the stuff. They made plans to get together Friday night.

Richard drove Therese to Vicki's apartment after supper and helped her carry her sleeping bag to the door. After Richard left, Vicki told Mr. Stern they were going to her room to listen to music. Mr. Stern was half asleep in his recliner in front of the blaring television. The girls didn't have to worry about him interfering in their business.

Vicki injected Therese and then herself using two different sterile needles. There was a slight pinch, and then a little burn, and then nothing. The two girls lay back on Vicki's bed and waited.

"I'm scared," Therese said.

"It's gonna be awesome," Vicki reassured her. "But this time, I'm jumping on the raft as soon as possible."

"Do you think we'll be able to see each other on the other side?" Therese asked.

"I hope so. If I see you, I'll grab your hand."

"Maybe we should hold hands now," Therese suggested.

"Um, sure, if you want."

Therese took Vicki's hand.

"Do you feel anything yet?" Vicki asked.

"I think so. Just a little. Oh."

"What?"

"I feel so peaceful."

"See what I mean? Oh. Now I feel it, too."

Therese could no longer speak, and she could only vaguely feel Vicki's hand in hers. She felt herself float up toward the ceiling, and now she looked down and saw her own body lying beside Vicki's on the bed. This is so weird. Then, right beside her on the ceiling, Vicki appeared holding her hand, but their bodies still lay on the bed. So, so weird, Therese thought again.

She decided to pray to Hermes, to tell him what she was up to. "I'm going to tell him off tonight, Hermes. I'm going to tell him how he broke my heart and how I never want to see him again. I'm going to the Underworld so I can tell him to his face."

She found herself in a dark tunnel. She couldn't see Vicki, but she could vaguely feel her hand in hers. A bright light shone at the end of the tunnel, so she half-walked, half-floated toward it. The walls of the tunnel looked like granite, and she wasn't sure, but she thought there was a very small spring running through the bottom of it. Her feet didn't feel wet, but she thought she could hear herself sloshing through the stream. When she finally reached the end of the tunnel, she recognized the Styx River in front of her. She was at the very same bank she had come to the night her parents were killed.

Fog curled around her, but she recognized the river flowing in a narrow gorge between two huge and creepy granite mountains. Her bare feet sunk into the itchy mud. She held on to Vicki, who stumbled beside her, to try and keep their balance. Tall blades of grass as high as their knees grew in tufts along the shore, tickling her bare legs. She wondered if she should have worn jeans and if it would have made a difference. She seemed to be in the shorts she had worn to Vicki's. Mosquitoes swarmed over one area of the water. Three large boulders leaned in a cluster on the left side of the shore against the base of a steep, massive wall of rock. Where was Charon?

Vicki tugged her across the sticky mud and tall blades of grass to the edge of the river, where Charon and his raft came into view. Without saying a word to the old, stooped man, Vicki jumped on board, pulling Therese with her.

Therese fought the urge to greet Charon by name as he gave them a look of confusion before towing them across.

The fog swirled around them like the tentacles of a gray octopus. Therese was surprised she wasn't cold or nervous. She felt completely at peace and couldn't wait to tell Than what she had come to say.

In fact, she felt so peaceful, that she found it hard to be angry. She had planned to scream her angry words, but the contentment swooned over her like a glittery beam of warm sunshine, and the anger dissipated into the fog.

She recognized Cerberus as they approached the huge black iron gate. She couldn't stop herself from saying sweetly, "Hey, boy. Hi there, Cerberus."

His three huge heads panted happily, and he wagged his long, dragon-like tail.

"You know him?" Vicki whispered.

Charon glared at them, so Therese said nothing.

The big gates creaked open, and Charon hovered just at the entrance.

"What are you waiting for?" Vicki asked the old man.

Then suddenly the contentment vanished from Therese, and she filled with dread as some kind of commotion took place around her. Cerberus's three huge heads barked ferociously. She couldn't quite tell what was happening, but she felt herself lifted away from the raft, and she could make out through the fog Charon leaving. She wondered if the drug could be wearing off so soon. Then someone shouted, "Grab her! Don't let her escape this time!" and big bodies were pushing and pulling Vicki away from her. Another had grabbed Therese and pulled her still further away from the gate. It was Hermes.

"You can't go through the gate," he said, panting from the struggle. "You'll piss off Hades for sure and never win his heart."

His wooly black hair blew in the gentle breeze up here away from the fog, far above the river. His dark eyes and dark beard were barely visible in what seemed to be obscured moonlight. His winged helmet gleamed, though, and so did his white teeth, which were gritted.

"It was foolish of you to come here. What made you think you could get away with this?"

Then she realized Vicki wasn't with them. "Where's my friend?"

Hermes shook his head but made no reply. Panic overcame Therese. She pushed herself free from Hermes and flew down to the gate. She saw Than holding Vicki against her will on the other side of the iron gate, which he was just now closing.

"Vicki!" Therese screamed, trying to push the gate open again. But it slammed shut in her face. "Than! Give me Vicki! She'll die!"

Than held on to Therese's struggling friend. "I'm sorry, Therese. Vicki has to stay here."

"No!" Therese threw herself against the iron bars of the gate, screaming at the top of her lungs. "No! Please! No! I beg you! I'll do anything! Take me instead!" She was tortured by the thought of Mr. Stern losing his only child on the heels of his wife's suicide. "I beg you, Than! If you love me, take me instead!"

"I have no choice. She's angered my father. She came through once before and cheated death. He won't let her do it again."

"But there's got to be a way! You can't let her die! Please! Her father will be so miserable! Please, Than!"

He shook his head again and backed away from the gate.

The anger Therese had felt over Than rekindled in her chest and she gave him a ferocious look. "I hate you, Thanatos! So you've been too busy to worry about me? The other night you were just doing your job? Well, I came down here to tell you to your face that I hate you and I never want to see you again! Stay out of my life! And send someone else to collect me when I'm dead!"

Hermes was there beside her now, trying to calm her down. He took her in his arms and allowed her blows to hit his chest rather than the iron bars of the gate. "I hate him!" she cried. Then she pleaded with Hermes, "Isn't there anything you can do to save my friend?"

"Even gods are limited by the will and actions of others. There's nothing I can do."

She looked through the gate at Than, who backed away, looking miserable. Vicki had stopped struggling, and her face reminded Therese of the blank expressions on her parents' faces the night she saw them in the Underworld. Therese realized Vicki must be dead already, and she wailed as loud as she could in the foggy air.

Than locked eyes with hers, his face contorted with pain. "When I said I'd been busy, I meant…"

But Hermes was pulling her back before she could hear the rest of Than's statement. Back they went from the river, from the muddy bank, through the dark granite tunnel. She floated for a brief moment on the ceiling and then popped back into her body. She opened her eyes and found Vicki lying beside her, dead.

Chapter Thirteen: The Labyrinth

Ariadne vanished, leaving Than alone at the entrance to the cavern, the labyrinth devised by Daedalus for King Minos centuries ago to house the Minotaur. In the old days, the Athenians sent seven warriors and seven maidens to be sacrificed to the Minotaur as payment for killing Minos's son, but once Theseus destroyed the Minotaur, that practice ended.

But the Minotaur was immortal, and he came back.

He had no regular food source, so he must depend on lost travelers for sustenance.

Although Than was immortal, he could be consumed by such a monster. And it would be painful. More threatening, though, was the recovery time. Than wasn't sure how long it would take, and his chances of securing Dionysus's help would be jeopardized. He would never see Therese as his bride.

Though now, as he crept through the winding, rocky maze, he feared he'd already lost her. The anger in her eyes when he kept her friend still haunted him. Why had Therese taken such a risk? Didn't she know she would lose his father's favor, which was already shaky if it existed at all? He was beginning to wonder if he was alone in still wanting this union. She hadn't really meant it when she said she hated him, had she?

Cracks in the rock above him allowed dim points of light to illuminate the passageway, adding to the light cast by his own body. Cables of different colors lay at his feet where others copied Theseus and his ball of yarn. He bent down and held a red colored chord and hoped to use it to find his way back. When he came to a fork in the tunnel, he recalled what Theseus, upon entering the Underworld, told him centuries

86

ago. He said, "One should go straight and down, never right or left." Than went straight and down.

He could easily god travel out of the labyrinth, as Ariadne well knew, but if she discovered it, she would refuse to help him. He could also disintegrate and hover above the labyrinth, making its outer walls transparent so he could guide his other self through, but he didn't want to risk Ariadne catching him at cheating. If he wanted Dionysus's help, he had to do this the hard way.

And since he carried no weapon, he would have to defend himself from the Minotaur with his bare hands.

Chapter Fourteen: Aftermath

Therese touched Vicki's limp body on the bed beside her, still warm. "Vicki?" She shook Vicki's shoulder. "Vicki?" She put her hand to Vicki's throat to feel for a pulse, her ear to Vicki's chest. Both were silent. This can't be happening. This must be a nightmare. Therese looked up to the ceiling and let out a blood-curdling scream.

Mr. Stern opened the bedroom door, his face at first bewildered. He might have said something, like "What's going on?" Then his expression changed to terror as he rushed to Vicki's side.

"Ducky? Talk to me, sweetheart!" He put his ear to her chest. "Ducky, love, wake up!"

Vicki did not move.

"Call 9-1-1," he said to Therese as he started CPR. "Now!"

"Oh my God!" she screamed, unable to think. Everything seemed to be happening in slow motion, but still her mind couldn't keep up. She stumbled around the bed for the phone on the nightstand and dialed the numbers, the same numbers she dialed around this same time last year.

She told the person on the other end the Stern's address. "She's not breathing! There's no pulse! Her dad's giving her CPR!" Her own voice kept asking her accusingly, *What have I done?*

"Stay on the line with me until someone arrives," the person on the other end said.

"I'm so sorry!" Therese didn't want to admit what they had done. "This wasn't supposed to happen." *What have I done?*

"Talk to me Therese," Mr. Stern said while he continued to pump Vicki's lifeless chest.

"She wanted to see her mom. She saw her last weekend using this drug. Ketamine. I wanted to see my parents, too. This wasn't supposed to happen." She couldn't breathe. She was hyperventilating. She didn't care. She wanted to die rather than face Mr. Stern.

The woman on the phone asked, "You and your friend took ketamine? Can you tell me how much and how long ago?"

Tears ran down Mr. Stern's sallow cheeks and some of the determination and hope vanished from his face. He stuck his finger down Vicki's throat. "I need to make her vomit." But Vicki's body would not respond.

Therese knew Hades would not let her return from the Underworld.

"This wasn't supposed to happen," she said again. In her mind, to Than, she said, "How could you?"

Mr. Stern rode in the ambulance with Vicki to the hospital while Carol, Richard, and Therese followed in Richard's car. Therese prayed to Hermes to please, please, please find a way to let Vicki return to the living. She couldn't stop crying and wished she herself could die. If she hadn't provided the money for the drugs, Vicki would be alive.

Carol and Richard weren't talking. They were so upset with her when they discovered what had happened: that Therese had bought the drug, had taken some herself, and not only contributed to the death of her friend but might have died herself.

Therese didn't blame them for being mad at her. She was mad at herself. She wished she, too, would have been taken by Death and forced to stay in the Underworld. The Lethe River was beginning to sound good.

"Hermes," she whispered too softly for the adults up front to hear. "You should have let me die."

Chapter Fifteen: The Minotaur

Straight and down, Than said to himself as he crept through the cave listening and watching for the first sign of the Minotaur. Ariadne had commanded Than to enter and exit the labyrinth, but she hadn't specified how far in he had to go. Couldn't he turn back now, especially since the red chord wound away, in the wrong direction, and he could no longer follow it?

No. He couldn't risk her denying him her help. He could tell she didn't want to go back to her husband, and he didn't want to make it easy for her to refuse him. He would go far into the belly of the beast, down and down, until he couldn't go any deeper. Once the path went uphill again, he'd know he was at its center.

He missed hearing Therese's voice. For ten months, her prayers had been constant, the only joy in his long life. He'd heard his father and other men joke about the tendency for women to talk more than most men, often to the point of annoyance, but Than looked forward to her daily prayers. Sometimes they were full of passion and longing, and his own longing would stir deep within him, nearly unbearable; but often they were clever remarks, funny comments and observations that would have him in stitches even as several thousand fragmented selves somberly escorted the dead. Therese had become the light of his existence. He didn't want to live without her.

But he couldn't hear her anymore. She stopped speaking to him. Hours had passed since he had taken Vicki to Erebus to lie in the pallid pool of the Lethe near her mother. In the interim between now and then, the only words to him from Therese were, "How could you?"

As he came upon a three-way fork in the passage, ignoring those to the left and right, he felt anger move through him. Therese knew he had no choice. It was unfair of her to blame him. Vicki had already gotten away with deceiving Hades once. She couldn't expect to do so twice.

Than had seen others like Vicki come to the gate in their drug-induced trip to jeer at him and Cerberus. Some had even boarded Charon's raft. But none had made it through the gate and gotten out alive save Vicki. It certainly couldn't happen twice. Therese had to know that. He was hurt she didn't seem more sympathetic to his point of view.

"How obtuse of her," he muttered.

No sooner had he made the remark than the Minotaur appeared before him, sprung from some crevice in the side of the rocky cavern. He gave Than no time for words, but shoved him with an unexpected force back against the wall. He hadn't been shoved like that since he and his brother wrestled together in the asphodel before they were old enough to take on their duties. Demigods had sometimes tried to shove him out of their way as they resisted death, but none were his match in strength. This Minotaur gave him pause. He'd forgotten exactly how the beast was immortal, though he sensed immortality was in his blood and not later conferred upon him. He stood up and pushed the monster back.

The Minotaur gasped when his humanoid back hit rock.

"I mean you no harm," Than said. "Let me pass through here, and I won't touch you again."

The beast panted as he pushed himself back to his feet and pointed the horns of his bull head at Than. "Oh, it's you. Why have you come? There are no dead nearby."

"Ariadne sent me."

"She sends only those she wishes to sacrifice to me. She knows how hungry I am. Why would she send a god to taunt my taste buds unless she meant for me to feast upon him?"

"Don't force me to kill you."

The Minotaur lunged for Than, who deftly moved and twisted in a flourish before the Minotaur could blink. The monster was strong, but he was no match in speed to the god of Death. Than pinned the beast's humanoid arms to his sides and again said, "I'm no Theseus, but I will kill you if you give me no choice."

His words seemed to further enrage the monster, who tucked his bull head down and butted Than's head. Than lost his grip on the beast and staggered back. Lighter on his feet, Than skipped past him, uphill and straight.

The path was not well-lit, but Than could see in the darkness and felt confident he would leave the beast in his dust. Then the Minotaur appeared before him and took him by surprise. He either used a shortcut or god traveled. After a moment's hesitation, Than ran into the monster with all his might and fell on him onto the narrow rocky ground of the passageway.

With the creature pinned beneath him, Than asked, "Why do you want to fight me? Are you really that hungry?"

The bull-man bucked Than from his torso, and Than fell on his back. Before the Minotaur could pin him, Than kicked the beast up against the ceiling. The beast and a cart load of rocks tumbled to the ground beside Than's feet. He jumped up and took the monster by the horns. "I hate to do this," he said, and with one twist, he broke the Minotaur's neck.

The body fell beneath Than as the soul emerged. Than put his hand on the beast's shoulder. "Tell me why. Was it really hunger? I could have brought you food."

"You came to take Ariadne."

"You love her?"

92

Ariadne appeared. "Asterion!" She glared at Than. "You killed him!"

"I had no choice." Than disintegrated so that one self could escort the beast's soul to the Underworld, though it wouldn't stay long.

"Wait!" Ariadne wrapped her arms around the transparent apparition of Asterion's soul. "I'll be waiting for you. I promise." Tears fell from her eyes. "I won't leave you again."

Than left with the soul to Charon while another disintegrated Than confronted the weeping goddess. "You promised you would return to Dionysus with me today."

"That was before you killed my brother."

"Brother?"

She looked up at him. "Our mother is the daughter of the sun-titan. She was tricked into sleeping with a white bull given to my father."

"I know your father. I didn't know you shared the same mother with the beast."

"He can't help what he is. Was."

"Is. As soon as his body regenerates, his soul will return. Though I don't understand how he's immortal if one parent was a bull."

"A magical bull from Poseidon, infused with Poseidon's blood."

"Great. I'm sure I just pissed off the god of the sea." He folded his arms across his chest. "Well, you'll have your brother back."

"Last time that took nearly a week."

"So go with me to Dionysus while you wait."

"Never. I couldn't bear for my brother to wake up here alone. I left him once to go with my husband, and before that, with Theseus, but never again. No one should have to live a life of solitude. It isn't fair."

Than wanted to say what his father had always said, "Life isn't fair, but death is," but he supposed that only applied to mortals. "Come with me now and return tomorrow."

"You know that won't happen. Dionysus has his methods of persuasion. Why do you suppose the maenads and satyrs never leave him? He'll trap me as he has before."

"You never meant to help me. So why did you send me into the maze?"

Ariadne lowered her eyes. "I was hurt when you rejected me. And now my brother suffers. Either comfort me in your arms or leave me before I rip my own eyes out as Oedipus once did."

"Goodbye, Ariadne." Than left her at once and entered his private chamber in the Underworld, not defeated by the Minotaur, but defeated nonetheless.

Chapter Sixteen: Saying Goodbye

Therese didn't want to attend Vicki's funeral, but Carol and Richard forced her to go. She sat between them on a hard wooden pew at St. Francis's Cathedral with a handful of others. The Holts sat in the pew in front of her. Ray and Todd were right behind her. A couple of teachers from Durango High were there. Mr. Stern slouched alone in the front pew. Therese felt the burden of his sadness. She could have stopped Vicki, should have stopped her, but had encouraged her for her own selfish reasons. Therese could meet no one's eyes, especially those of Mr. Stern's. This was mostly her fault. She pondered the bottle of sleeping pills and Prozac in her medicine cabinet. If she took both bottles of pills, would that be enough to kill her?

The funeral mass was the longest service of Therese's life. She could feel the cold, hard, accusing eyes glancing her way. When news spread about what had happened, Therese received a lot of cold looks. Even Jen was outraged, though she had enough heart not to say so. She didn't need to. Therese could see it in her friend's eyes. The only person in Therese's life who showed sympathy instead of judgment was Pete Holt.

At the graveside service, her despair and remorse over everything—the loss of her parents, the loss of Than, the loss of Puffy and Dumbo, and now of Vicki, whom she might have saved had she been responsible enough—shuddered through her body in uncontrollable sobs. She stood behind the metal folding chairs, outside of the canopy, several feet behind Carol and Richard, not wanting to be seen, sunglasses shielding her swollen eyes, when Pete Holt approached from behind and took her hand. He squeezed it, and this small act of kindness sent her into hysterics. He took her in his arms and held her as she wept, allowing herself to collapse in his arms.

After a brief reception at Mr. Stern's apartment, where a few people brought food Mr. Stern would probably never eat, Pete came over and sat with Therese in the swing on her wooden deck where they watched the sunset across Lemon Reservoir. They rocked back and forth, holding hands, saying nothing, and it was nice.

But it wasn't long before Therese's thoughts went to Than. As angry as she was for his role in Vicki's death, and despite her own miserable feelings of guilt, her heart continued to ache for him against her will. She hated herself for that. Why couldn't she love Pete? He was everything she could want in a guy. He was gorgeous, sweet, funny, and smart. And she could tell how much he loved her. Maybe she could learn to love him back.

As if he sensed her thoughts, Pete lifted her chin, looked into her eyes, and said, "Can I kiss you?"

She slowly nodded and closed her eyes.

Pete's warm lips softly swept against hers, but instead of exalting, she filled with dread. This wasn't right. She carried out the kiss and waited for him to end it, but inside, she thought it couldn't end too quickly.

He looked at her with a smile. "That was nice."

"Yes, it was."

He kissed her again, and she bore it, convincing herself it was the right thing to do. How had she ever thought she could marry Death and become a god?

That night, alone in her room, after Carol and Richard had come to talk to her about making good choices—on the heels of her friend's funeral, really?—she took out her flute and played a tribute to Hermes. As she played a piece by Bach, she sang in her mind her prayer to him: "Help me, Hermes. Help me find a way either to fall out of love with Than or to be with him. I can't take this agony. Maybe it's time for me to join my parents. Maybe it's time for me to die, too. Please, Hermes. All my hopes lie with you." She continued to play and to meditate on these thoughts as tears rolled down her cheeks until she was too tired to go on.

Chapter Seventeen: Another Deal with Hades

Than appeared before his father near the flames of the Phlegethon River illuminating the vast private chamber where Hades spent most of his time. Hades sat on a chaise lounge and held a book in his hand, but he wasn't looking at it. He was speaking with Alecto, who stood close by, her python wrapped around her waist and lying over one shoulder. They both looked at Than when he appeared.

"Am I interrupting?"

"We were just discussing you," Hades remarked. "Alecto believes a recent soul taken to Erebus must be vindicated."

"Who?"

"Vicki Stern." Alecto stepped forward and squared herself to her brother. "Your old girlfriend is partly to blame."

"How? She didn't force or persuade the other girl to take the drug."

"She bought the drug." Alecto's eyes turned as red as her hair, and one drop of blood dripped onto her cheek. "She's culpable."

Great. Alecto's charge wouldn't help Than's case. "I came here to tell you of an important decision I've made. Whatever the consequences, I'm determined to make Therese a god."

Alecto gasped.

Hades jumped from his chair. "Are you mad?"

"I guess that means I won't be getting your blessing."

Hades stepped closer. "The maenads will rip you to pieces once a year forever."

Like he didn't already know that. Than resisted the urge to say this sarcastic thought out loud. "I want this."

Hades started to say something, but then didn't. He sat back down in his chair and put his chin in one hand. Than waited quietly for several seconds and was about to speak again, when his father said, "I have an idea."

Alecto moved to her father's side. "You can't be seriously considering a way to..."

"This idea will settle your issues as well."

"I'm listening," Than said.

"We give her five challenges, as penance for her role in the girl's death and as a means for proving she's worthy to become like us. If she succeeds, I'll use all my power to force Dionysus to make her a god. Then you'll be spared the maenads."

"What kind of challenges?" Than's heart sank. This didn't sound good.

"They need to prove she has what it takes. We need to know if she's trustworthy, diplomatic, yet cunning. She has to be strong and brave."

"So we're holding her to higher standards than we do the rest of us."

Hades laughed. "To be sure, though I know you don't include me among those whom you see lacking."

"That goes without saying."

Hades searched Than's face for signs of sarcasm, but Than showed none.

"What do you have in mind, Father?" Alecto asked.

Hades sat silent for a moment, thinking, while his son and daughter waited. Than stared off into the flames of the Phlegethon, silently begging his father to consider his happiness.

Then Hades stood up, and, pacing with excitement, said, "To prove she's trustworthy, we'll have her deliver a black box from

Aphrodite to Persephone containing a beauty charm which Therese is not to open. Aphrodite asked this of Cupid's Psyche and countless others, and even though the women were already beautiful, they couldn't resist stealing a little more beauty for themselves. We'll see if Therese can resist what others could not."

Than sighed with relief, feeling confident Therese would not falter. She was anything but vain.

"For her second challenge," Hades said, "to test her skills in diplomacy, she must deliver to Mount Olympus one of Hera's golden apples, guarded in her orchard by the Hesperides and Ladon, the one-hundred-headed dragon."

"How do you expect her to get by the dragon?" Than demanded. "You know it's impossible."

"It wasn't for Hercules."

"She won't be long in finding her way here," Than said. "But not as my bride."

"You have little faith in the girl you love," Alecto sneered.

Than shook his head, his ears thudding with the beat of his heart. His father must not care for him, he thought bitterly. He clenched his jaw and turned away to leave.

"Don't you want to hear what the other three challenges are?" Hades asked.

"To humor you, Father?"

"Indeed."

"I'm listening," he spat angrily.

"The third will test her cunning," Hades said. "For that I want her to negotiate through the Labyrinth."

Both the Minotaur and his sister Ariadne were no friends to Than. If by some miracle Therese made it past the one-hundred-headed dragon, they would kill Therese.

"You are not allowed to intervene," Hades said, as if reading his thoughts. "If you want to train her for battle, you may. You may even offer advice. The actual challenges she must endure alone."

Than glared at his father.

"For strength, she must defeat the Hydra."

Than laughed. "This is ridiculous."

"And for courage, she must descend into the Underworld, find Vicki Stern, and apologize to her."

"Why such an easy task on the heels of the others?" Than asked. "You know she can't defeat the dragon, the Minotaur, and the Hydra, so you throw that last one in there for grins?"

"The last is the most difficult of all," Hades replied. "Because like Orpheus, she won't be allowed to look back."

"She can do that, but it doesn't matter. You've set her up for failure."

Alecto stepped closer to Than, "Don't be too quick to give up."

As much as Than appreciated his sister's encouragement, he said, "Never mind, then, Father. I'll do it without your blessing. I want her alive."

"Wait, brother," Alecto said. "At least give her the choice."

Chapter Eighteen: The Impossible Dream

After Pete left, Therese went straight through the house and up the stairs to her room, hoping neither her aunt nor her uncle would follow. She wanted to be alone. Except for her pets, she didn't want company.

She changed into an old pair of sweats she usually wore in the winter, hoping they would help her body stop trembling. She held Jewels against her neck, the shell warm from its heat lamp. Then she wished the tortoise goodnight, turned off the lamp, and crawled beneath her covers. As exhausted as she was, she lay in bed beside Clifford unable to fall asleep.

"Oh, Clifford," she muttered. "What am I going to do?"

He nudged the palm of her hand with his head, which meant, "Pet me," so she scratched behind his ears and along his back. He rolled over for a belly scratch. Stroking him released some of the anxiety that had built up inside of her. Her neck and shoulders loosened a little, and she sank further into her pillow. She closed her eyes and continued to pet Clifford until she finally drifted off to sleep.

Therese found herself walking through a neighborhood, lost. It was her grandparents' neighborhood, in San Antonio. She used to ride a bike around these blocks during visits, but she'd never gotten lost. Why couldn't she find her way now? She turned a corner and headed up another block. Some of the houses slanted in odd angles to the ground. This is weird, she thought. She'd never seen houses like this before.

She was dreaming.

She kicked off the ground and swam the breast stroke through the air, flying above the treetops. She flipped onto to her back and floated, wondering why her grandparents' old neighborhood had been in her dream and why she had gotten lost in it. Before long, she felt another presence floating near her.

It was a figment disguised as Than. She turned to face it, her body stiff with anger. Even though she knew it was just a stupid figment, she couldn't stop the heat from rising to her skin and the words to her throat. "Get away from me!"

"Therese, please." The figment moved closer, touching a hand to her cheek.

She looked at him with longing, but the fact that he could be this close and not cause her to grow weak with dying proved he was just a stupid figment. She pressed her palms against his bare chest and pushed. "Get away!" she growled.

"No. Not until you've heard me out. If you still want me to go then, I will."

"Figment, I command you to show yourself!"

Than moved closer, taking her hand. "I'm not a figment. It's me."

She jerked back, eyes wide. "What?" Her heart pounded in her ears. She wasn't sure whether she was mad or happy. Maybe a little of both. "What are you doing here? How come I'm not dying?"

He ran a hand through her short hair. "I like your hair this way."

Her mouth went dry, her palms moist. "Why are you here?"

"My father ordered Hip to trade places with me for the night. I need to talk to you."

"And you couldn't manage this months ago?" Her voice came out harsh and bitter. She regretted it as soon as she saw his face.

"I've been trying, believe me. Can we please sit down somewhere and talk?"

She folded her arms across her chest, unsure. Seeing him made her knees weak; she could barely maintain herself in the air because her body felt wobbly, her heart unsteady. Yes, she wanted to sit down, but should she talk to him? After what he did to Vicki? The idea of *not* talking to him made her stomach ache. "Okay. Where?"

He took her hand and led her down through the clouds, down through tall granite peaks, down into a ravine where a river flowed, down to the gate of the Underworld.

"I thought I wasn't allowed to enter," she said, suddenly terrified. Was he planning to kill her?

"Not through there. I'm taking you around back, to a secret entrance to my rooms. You can only enter through the dream world."

They ran across a field of poppies. Lying amid the flowers on his back with his eyes closed was Than.

"Wait a minute," she said. "Is that you?" She pointed to his sleeping form a few feet away from them.

"That's how I enter the dream world."

"So this isn't the real you?" She touched his chest. It felt good to touch him.

He covered her hand and held it against him. "It's as much the real me as it is the real you. Hard to explain. Just come on."

He led her inside a dome-shaped cavern with high ceilings and a river of fire. A grouping of instruments hung above the flames on one wall. Across from the river was a fireplace, also alight with flames, and arranged in front of it were two leather club chairs. In the center of the room, a table and two chairs looked like they were carved from gold.

"Welcome to my home," he said, his cheeks turning red. "Come, sit down."

Therese looked around in awe, the dome ceiling, curved high above them, reminding her of a cathedral. She took a seat across from him near the fire place in the cozy leather chair. "It's nice."

"You really like it?"

104

"Yes. I do." She looked up again at the ceiling, where their shadows danced.

Than gave her his adorable smile and leaned toward her, sitting on the edge of his seat. She sat forward, too, so their knees touched, her knees pressed together inside of his. She pressed them together to keep them from shaking. He took one of her hands, holding it on her thigh, hot beneath her sweats.

"I can't believe you're really here," he said. "I've fantasized about this for months."

"Why *am* I here? What's this all about?" She couldn't keep the resentment from her tone. He should have come for her months ago.

He told her all about his efforts to make her into a god in spite of the oath he and the Olympians took last summer. He told her about Aphrodite, about the maenads, about Dionysus, and about Ariadne and the Minotaur. As he spoke, the iron glove around her heart melted away. She put a hand to her mouth, taking it all in. He hadn't been too busy for her; he'd been busy *because* of her. She felt like a fool. She closed her eyes to hold in the tears, but they fell down her cheeks anyway.

He smoothed the tears away with his thumbs. "Don't cry."

"I'm so sorry I lost faith in you," she muttered. "I thought you didn't love me anymore. I thought once you returned to your duties, you realized you'd made a mistake, that I wasn't anything special, that you didn't want me."

"No." He stood and pulled her from the chair and into his arms. "No way."

She put her cheek against his chest and let him hold her. Even though she knew this was a dream, she also knew it was real, and it felt real. She could feel the rise and fall of his chest with each breath, could hear his heart pumping against her cheek.

105

He stroked her hair. "You know I had no choice but to take Vicki, right? You understand that?"

She looked into his eyes. "It was my fault, not yours. Besides, Hades makes no exceptions, does he," she said without inflection. "And you are under his command."

"Exactly."

"Have you ever disobeyed your father?"

He shook his head. "But I will if necessary, to be with you."

"Oh, Than."

He pulled her hard against him and kissed the top of her head, then cupped her chin in his hand and lifted her face to his. She met his eyes, and her body responded to the longing she recognized in them, the longing she knew her eyes also held. Softly, she whispered, "I can't believe this is happening."

"Believe it," he said, just before he covered her mouth with his.

She took his lips in hers, licking, sweeping, tasting. She couldn't resist taking his lower lip between her teeth and gently biting down.

"Mmm," he groaned.

He lifted her up in his arms and carried her from the room into another, following the river of fire, past a stalagmite holding a clock and quill to a round bed beneath a golden sword and shield. Next to the bed was a trickling waterfall cascading over a series of shelves carved from stone and displaying a beautiful shell collection. Three green plants, somewhat transparent, grew in pots beside the waterfall, and though Therese was amazed by the room, and able to take in every detail with the slow motion of a dream, she closed her eyes when Than laid her on his bed and kissed her. He climbed beside her, half on top of her, and cupped her head in his hands, lifting her face to his. The soft, sweeping, gentle kisses became hard and passionate and deep. Therese wrapped her arms around his neck and lifted her body against his.

His hand moved to her cheek, along her chin, down her neck, and gently caressed her collarbone at the top of her sweatshirt.

A moan escaped her lips as she slipped one hand from his neck and circled it around his back, pressing him to her. She tugged his dark wavy hair, pulling his lips harder against hers. Then she stopped, full of panic, and looked, wide-eyed, at Than. Were they going to have sex? She wasn't so sure she was ready for that, even in a dream.

"Therese? What's wrong?"

"I, it's just that, you can't get pregnant from a dream, right?"

His eyes burned with desire. In a low, steady voice, he said, "Right."

"Does that mean you, I mean, are we going to, you know?" She swallowed air, then sucked in her lips.

He smiled down at her. "We're not doing anything you're not ready for."

She hadn't realized she was holding her breath, but she let the air out now.

"Okay?" he asked.

"Okay."

He kissed her again and held her in his arms. "Besides, we still need to talk. I have something serious to discuss with you."

He rolled onto his back with his arm beneath her shoulders. She nestled in the crook of his arm, her cheek against his warm bare chest, her palm against his ripped abdomen. She'd never touched him like this, so freely, probably because she felt less inhibited in the dream world than in the real. She caressed his belly, feeling the muscle tone, every ripple, just above his waistband.

He moaned and stopped her hand, lacing his fingers into hers.

"What are you thinking?" she prayed. "Talk to me."

His answer came to her mind without him uttering it. He said, "I'm going to make you a god so you can come down here and be with me forever. But it's going to hurt. Really bad."

She gasped and prayed, "How did you do that? Communicate with me without talking?"

"This is a dream. The rules are different."

"Oh."

"You know Vicki would have taken the ketamine with or without you, don't you?"

"She didn't have the money. I don't know."

"She would have found a way."

"Maybe."

He stroked her hair and then her cheek. "Would you want to live here with me?"

"Yes."

"My grandmother knows a way. See, only Zeus can confer immortality on a human the normal way on Mount Olympus—where a mortal can drink ambrosia—but without Zeus's power, we have to use a more painful method. I'll understand if you can't do it. To be honest, I've had my doubts about asking you."

"What is it?"

"I'll take you to my grandmother's winter cabin where I'll anoint your body with ambrosia—to drink it without Zeus would kill you. Then I'll light your body on fire."

"What?"

"And your mortal body will burn to death as your immortal body rises from the ashes."

"Are you serious?"

"You don't have to do it. Forget it."

"No. I want to." Therese tried not to let the terror into her thoughts as she wondered if she could allow herself to be set on fire, if she could endure being burnt alive. She shivered at the thought, silently gasping for air, and tears came to her eyes. Though she doubted herself, though she worried at the last moment she would run away from it, she prayed to Than, "I can do it. I'd do anything to be with you. But what about the maenads?"

He put a hand on her cheek and looked into her eyes. "It's like you said: I'd do anything for you. I don't care about that. Once a year, what's that compared to an eternity without you?"

She gave him a sad smile. "Will your father allow this?"

As they lay quietly stroking one another, he told her what his father had proposed. He'd give them his blessing and aid, forcing Dionysus to help, if she proved herself worthy. He described the five challenges.

She sat up and spoke out loud, "You don't think I can do it!"

He sat up, too. "You think you can?"

She hopped off the bed and paced around the room. "No. But I want you to believe I can. Maybe I can. Maybe I can."

"No mortal can. He's giving you a set of impossible tasks to punish you for what you did last summer on Mount Olympus." He moved to the edge of the bed.

"If I fight the dragon, the Minotaur, and the Hydra, you'll be spared. Right? With Dionysus's help, the maenads will leave you alone."

He nodded. "Don't do it, Therese. At least, if we do it ourselves, your life won't be in danger. I can't risk losing you."

"But it's my choice, right? You'll honor my decision?"

He nodded again and took her in his arms. He sat on the bed with his feet on the floor and his legs spread open. She stood between his

109

knees and held his head against her belly while he circled her waist with his arms.

"But please, think seriously about this," he said with his cheek against her sweatshirt. "I promise I can handle the maenads. If you can endure the fire…"

"But that's one time, Than. The maenads will rip you to pieces every year for, like, forever."

He lifted his eyes to hers, his chin against her stomach. "I only told you about the five challenges because Alecto said the choice should be yours, and she's right. But please don't make a hasty decision. You'll break my heart if you die."

She ran her fingers through his hair and kissed his forehead. "I won't let myself die."

He sighed. "Do you know how many times I've heard that right before I've led a soul here?"

"I won't let it happen. I'll think of something. I can feel it. You and I were meant to be together, I know it. I tried to love Pete. I'm sorry, but I did. And it felt so wrong. So wrong. And this, between you and me, it feels like it was always meant to be. So I can't die. I can't."

He stood up and pulled her into him. "I love you."

She looked up at him, feeling brave for the first time in her life, feeling more determined than ever to achieve something she wanted. "I . . ." But before she could utter her thought, she woke up in her bed next to Clifford, and Than was gone.

Tossing and turning and checking her clock every few minutes for over an hour, she couldn't stand the idea that this was her one night with Than and she couldn't get to him because she couldn't fall asleep. "Help me," she finally prayed. "Help me fall asleep."

He appeared beside her, shocking her. She hadn't expected him to come.

"My presence won't kill you," he said, stroking her cheek. "But it will make you . . ."

Before he could complete his sentence, she was back in the dream, only now on the bed beside him.

"Tell me what you were about to say," he whispered.

They lay against one another on his round bed facing each other with the waterfall trickling beside them. The glimmer from the river of fire sparkled in Than's eyes.

"I was going to say, I love you, too."

They held one another in the dream world for the rest of the night, but at dawn, Than kissed her once more and vanished. She found herself floating in the clouds above her grandparents' old neighborhood. Hip appeared beside her.

"He had to go back to guide the dead, but I'll hang out with you, if you'd like."

"Do you know about the five challenges?"

"Yeah. You've got to try, Therese. Don't let the maenads have my brother."

"I'm going to try. I'm going to try my hardest. Your dad said I had to do it alone, but he didn't say I couldn't use the gifts I already have, right? I can use Aphrodite's traveling robe and Artemis's invisibility crown. I wonder where the sword and shield are that Hephaestus made me last summer."

"I'll find out." He moved closer. "Hey, you're waking up."

She opened her eyes to the bright sunlight streaming into her room, and though she was frightened of what lay ahead, she also felt excited to finally have some control over her own destiny.

Chapter Nineteen: Than Prepares

Than should have known Therese would choose to fight for him, but he wasn't going to stand by and let her die. He would hover from a safe distance, so as not to drain her life force, and the moment she was mortally injured, he would carry her off to his grandmother.

He stood outside the palace at Mount Olympus and said, "Spring, Summer, Winter, and Fall, open the gates of Olympus so I, Thanatos, may enter."

A loud roar carried through the air, and a tunnel of cold wind lifted in front of him. As the wind settled and the rain cloud emptied its contents and dissipated, the giant wall of clouds opened, and Than stepped through. The wall of clouds closed behind him as he crossed the golden-paved plaza and passed the fountain spraying water beneath a rainbow from the spout of a golden whale. He took the rainbow steps, passed the marble columns, and entered the palace.

He was on his way to see Hephaestus to ask after Therese's sword and shield and had put his hand on the knob to the forge when the sound of voices raised in anger coming from the courtroom made him pause.

A movement across the foyer caught his eye, and he turned to see Hestia clearing dishes from the dining room table. She put a finger to her lips and beckoned him inside.

He crossed the foyer, and once beside her, asked, "What's going on in there?"

"Alecto's been here. She told your mother about the five challenges. She also told her about your desire to make Therese a god without Dionysus's help."

"They know I plan to break my oath."

"That's not all. Persephone went to Zeus and begged him to intervene by convincing your father to forget about the challenges. She wants Zeus to force Dionysus to help you. She's so upset with Hades. But Zeus sees no reason to contradict him. Ares got wind of it, and now he's offended that Hades would work in league with Dionysus against him. He's against the challenges, too, but for different reasons than your mother."

For most of his life, Than was spared from the constant conflict among the gods at Mount Olympus, one of the few advantages of dwelling in the Underworld; but now he found himself the center of their attention, and he didn't like it. Why should they control his fate? He was tired of being another cog in the wheel. He wouldn't stand for it. He thanked Hestia and swiftly left the room to confront the other gods.

When Than entered the court, the room became quiet and all eyes turned to him. Every throne was occupied except for those belonging to Hades and Poseidon, who spent their time in their respective palaces beneath the world and sea. Before Than could speak his mind to those present, Zeus spoke in his angry, earth-quaking voice.

"If you break your oath on the River Styx, Thanatos, you will never be allowed to enter these palace walls again. Do you understand?"

So they would exile him. Wasn't he already exiled most of the time? "I understand, Lord Zeus, but my problem could be remedied if Dionysus would do me the favor. He took no oath." Than glanced at Aphrodite, who quickly turned her gaze to the marble floor.

"If Hades hadn't already made this deal with you, I might have intervened, but now I can't risk turning my brother against me over this minor matter."

Than looked across the room at his mother and grandmother, seated on their double throne. His mother was in tears, his grandmother holding her hand and comforting her.

113

"Can't you just forget this girl?" Artemis suddenly said.

He knew the virgin goddesses would never understand him, so he turned to Aphrodite and Hera, natural enemies most of the time, and silently prayed to them. "Aphrodite, goddess of love, stand by me. Queen Hera, patron of all wives and mothers, feel my aching heart."

Hera's face softened. Than thought she would speak, but it was Hermes who crossed the room to Than's side. "These two lovers won't give up. Therese is willing to fight for Thanatos. I say let her. Thanatos is willing to accept the consequences of breaking his oath. What more is there to say? If he'll withstand the maenads and exile for the rest of eternity, justice will be served."

Persephone stood from her throne. "Justice? I'm so sick of justice! What happened to mercy? Two souls love one another. Why can't we let them be happy?"

Aphrodite stood and said, "Hear, hear!"

The room roared with angry voices until Zeus's thundering growl silenced them. "To answer your question, Persephone, there are too many interests at stake. The girl had her chance to avenge her parents' death last summer. She made her choice. The court agreed on a plan of action. The power of this court would be undermined if we didn't uphold its decisions."

"Hear, hear!" Ares said, mocking Aphrodite with a mischievous smile.

"This discussion is over," Zeus commanded. He stood from his throne and left the room by way of his chamber door, directly behind his throne.

Than went to his mother and grandmother. "Trust me. Don't make any more trouble for me here."

"The thought of my son being torn to pieces every year..."

"Please, Mother." He kissed the top of her head and then crossed the room to Hephaestus.

"Sir, you made a sword and shield for Therese last summer. Do you know what became of them?"

Hephaestus put a hand on Than's shoulder, smiled kindly—his ugly, misshapen face taking on a kind of beauty—and said, "I have them in my forge. I recovered them from the battleground. I don't like to see my handiwork wasted. Listen, I'm sorry for your troubles. And if there's anything I can do to help, I will. I hate that dastardly god of war, for reasons I'm sure you know, and like my wife, I like to see lovers united in marriage."

Than smiled for the first time that day.

Chapter Twenty: The Little Black Box of Beauty

Therese climbed out of bed, recalling the dream. As she turned on Jewels's lamp and headed to her bathroom, she thought it was probably just an ordinary dream—a nice one, the best, but ordinary. It reminded her that her heart belonged to Than no matter how hard she tried to love Pete. But when she climbed beneath the warm water of the shower, the realness of the dream came back to her. Than had come to her in the dream world. They spent the night together in his room. He told her what he'd been doing to get them together again—about the maenads, Dionysus, and the Minotaur. He told her about the five challenges. The determination she felt when she had first awakened returned. It hadn't been an ordinary dream, and she was eager to get started.

She rinsed the shampoo from her hair and prayed to Than, "I miss you already. It won't be long. I promise. I'll start today."

After her shower, she dressed and went downstairs to take Clifford outside. Carol and Richard sat at the granite breakfast bar eating bowls of cereal. Therese had been avoiding them since Vicki's death, but she knew they wanted to talk to her more about what had happened. She hoped it wouldn't be today. She didn't want anything to sour her mood and dampen her determination to face the five challenges. She gave them a smile and said, "Good morning," on her way out the back door.

Once in the woods, she prayed to Aphrodite, asking her to bring her the little black box, or to tell her where she should go to find it. Following Clifford up the trail into the woods behind her house, where the birds chirped and flitted from tree to tree and an occasional chipmunk scrambled across her path, she looked for signs of the goddess.

116

"Come on, Clifford," she said when he stopped to sniff the grass. "Let's keep going."

She heard a rustle in the brush ahead of her and froze. In her mind, she asked, "Aphrodite?" though she expected to see a deer. She heard the rustle again, and studied the brush in front of her. She could see no signs of an animal but definitely sensed a presence.

"Hello?" Therese said meekly.

A figure appeared before her, but it wasn't Aphrodite; it was Jen. She held the invisibility crown in one hand and wiped tears from her eyes with the back of the other.

"Jen? What's wrong?"

"Same old, same old." Her voice quivered as she spoke.

"Your dad?"

Jen nodded.

Clifford noticed her from across the trail and ambled over to greet her.

Jen leaned down to pet him and gave him a smile. "Hi, Clifford."

"You wanna talk?" Therese asked.

"Sure. Can we go to your room?"

"Come on."

They took the trail down through the forest, past the elms, when Therese noticed a little black box, the size of a Rubik's Cube, on the wooden deck. She picked it up, her heart pounding.

"What's that?" Jen asked.

"I'm not sure."

"Open it."

Therese clamped the lid tight. "Not now. Come on."

They entered the house through the back door, by the kitchen. Carol and Richard stood at the sink rinsing out their breakfast bowls.

"Can Jen come over for a while?" Therese asked.

117

"What about breakfast?" Carol asked. "Are you hungry, Jen?"

"No thanks."

"I'm not either," Therese added.

Carol glanced up at Richard, who nodded and said, "Let us know when you're hungry, and we'll fix you something, okay?"

"Thanks."

The two girls skipped up the stairs followed by Clifford. Therese put the wooden box in a dresser drawer, hoping Jen would ask no more about it. "So tell me what's going on," she asked as she refilled Clifford's food and water bowls and added more water to Jewels's tank.

Jen sat on the bed, cradling the crown. "My dad won't stop drinking again. My mom keeps threatening to throw him out, but I don't believe her. She likes having him around to help with the ranch. It makes me feel like she loves him more than she does me." Tears poured from Jen's eyes.

Therese sat beside her on the bed, unable to imagine how Jen must feel. Therese's parents would never have hurt her or put her in harm's way. She shivered at their memory, and her longing to be with them resurfaced. Therese shoved it back down and swallowed. "She probably doesn't know what to do. She's human. And humans make mistakes and don't always know the right answers. Have you thought about calling someone, like a social worker?"

"I'm afraid they'll take me and Bobby away. I'd rather stay and use the crown."

"Has it helped then?"

Jen nodded. "I don't know what I'd do without it. I sleep on the floor in my closet with it on every night. I pin it to my hair so it won't fall off. He's only come in my room once, but still. It was terrifying. He acts like he just wants a hug, but when he's drunk, he doesn't know how to stop." Jen shuddered and put on the crown. "Don't look at me."

118

Therese lowered her gaze to the floor. "I'm so sorry. I don't know what to say except that I'm glad the crown helps."

Jen took it off. "How does it work? Where did you get it?"

"I told you not to ask."

"Please? I've just told you the worst secret ever. Can't you tell me yours?"

Therese considered Jen's question. Could she trust Jen not to tell a soul if she told her everything about Than and the other gods? It would be nice to have someone, someone human, to talk to. "Well," her stomach lurched. She couldn't risk it. She couldn't risk spoiling her chances to be with Than. "There's no real secret, Jen. Someone gave it to me. I think she was my guardian angel. I'm not sure. Maybe my mom."

"You could have kept it for yourself."

"You need it more right now. But I might need to take it back, for a short while."

"Why?"

"Not today. But maybe soon. I'll give it right back."

"You're not going to tell me why?"

"Do I have to?"

Jen shook her head. "You aren't going to take any more drugs, are you?"

"No." Therese's stomach felt sick as she thought of Vicki.

"Why'd you do it?"

"She wanted to see her mom. I wanted to see my parents." Therese bit the inside of her lip.

"That's crazy."

"I know."

Jen looked up at Therese and put a hand on her shoulder. "Thanks for loaning me the crown. I don't know what I'd do without it."

Therese hugged her friend. "You're welcome."

119

"Now let's open that box," Jen stood up and went to the dresser drawer, opening it.

Therese leapt across the room, her chest tight, her heart pounding. "No!" She reached for the box. For one horrible split second, the box slipped from the hands of both girls and dangerously dropped through the air. Therese gasped and caught it just before it hit the floor.

"You don't know what you almost did." Therese looked at Jen with wide eyes. Her future life with Than would have vanished from the realm of possibility.

"What? What's in there?"

Therese thought quickly. "My parents' ashes."

"I didn't know they were cremated. They fit in that?"

"Yeah."

"Then why were they out on the deck?"

"The box got wet, and I wanted to put it in the sun to dry."

"Then why did you act like you didn't know what it was?"

"I didn't want you to know I like to carry the box around. It makes me feel closer to my parents."

"Oh." Jen sat on the bed. "Don't be embarrassed about that. Okay?"

"Okay. Thanks."

"Are you coming to groom Stormy today?"

"After lunch."

Relief swept over Therese once Jen left. The thought of what had almost happened made her tremble. She set the box on her dresser, afraid to hold it in her quaking hands, moving it to the center, away from the edges, staring at it. Now what was she supposed to do? She silently prayed to Persephone and Aphrodite for further instructions.

Two figures appeared on either side of her. Boys. Twins. They had deep red hair, long and thick like the mane of a lion, and fierce black eyes. They were beautiful, but they frightened her.

She took a step back, sucking in her lips, her heart speeding beneath her ribs. Clifford cowered beside her with his paws over his eyes.

"I'm Phobos," one of them said. "And this is my brother, Deimos."

"We're sons of Aphrodite," Deimos explained.

Clifford started whining.

"Aphrodite?" Therese wanted to be grateful, wanted to believe they were there to help her, but fear choked her and panic gave her the shakes. "I-I-I'm Therese. It's..." She fought the irrational terror taking hold of her. She wanted to attack the boys with her bedside lamp. How crazy was that? "A pleasure to meet you." The air rushed from her body. She clinched her hands together to keep them from trembling and to keep them from flailing out.

The two brothers exchanged looks of surprise and laughed.

"A pleasure to meet us?"

"Us?"

"Y-y-es. I adore your mother." She wanted to flee from the room. She couldn't breathe. In her mind, she screamed, "Help!" to Than, to Hermes, to anyone who'd listen. "Help me, please!"

The boys frowned.

"It's never a pleasure to meet us."

"You're lying."

"Try-trying t-to be p-p-polite!"

"Have you ever taken a good look at yourself in the mirror?" Phobos asked. "You could use a pick-me-up."

"The beauty charm in our mother's box could serve you well, ugly. Think Than wants a plain girl like you at his side?"

Therese backed into the corner of her room. "Go away!" The panic and fear claimed her heart, erratic and mad, adrenaline pumping through every vein in her trembling body. She screamed. The twins laughed. She screamed again.

The door to her room swung open, the twins vanished, and Carol and Richard rushed in.

"Therese!" Carol cried. "What's happening?"

Therese gaped at them.

"Therese?" Richard asked. "You okay?"

"I'm not sure."

"What made you scream?" Carol asked.

"I don't know. I think maybe I was having a nightmare. Maybe I was sleepwalking just now. I don't know."

Carol and Richard exchanged worried glances.

"Why don't you come downstairs and watch a little TV with us, sweetheart?" Carol suggested. "I'll make you some hot tea."

Therese glanced at the black box on her dresser. Carol followed her gaze.

"Oh, what's that?" Carol asked, crossing the room and taking the box in her hands.

"Don't open it!" Therese shouted. "Put it down!"

Carol did not put down the box, but instead looked Therese hard in the eye and asked, "Then tell me what's in it."

"A gift."

"For whom?"

"Uh, I, um, Jen."

"Then why didn't you give it to her earlier?"

Richard took the box from Carol. "This better not be drugs. Are there drugs in here? Were you hallucinating just now?"

"No! No! I promise! I'm not taking drugs."

Richard cupped the bottom of the box in one hand and the lid in the other.

"Don't!"

He pulled the lid from the box.

Therese dropped to her knees. It was over, her life with Than forever out of reach.

Richard and Carol looked inside.

"Oh," Carol said. "A ring. It's lovely. For Jen?"

Therese lifted her eyes and examined her aunt and uncle. They looked unchanged. Why hadn't the beauty charm escaped and transformed them? Not that they weren't already attractive people. "Um…"

Carol plucked the ring from the box and held it up in the light. "Is it silver? Or white gold?"

Therese stared at the thin metal band, wondering if the charm only worked when the ring was placed on a person's finger. "Silver." Please don't put it on, she thought. Please.

Carol closed her eyes for a moment and sighed. When she opened them again, she asked, "Did this belong to your mom?"

Not knowing what else to do, Therese nodded.

"There's nothing wrong with giving it to Jen. Did you think I'd be upset?"

Therese nodded again.

Carol tucked it back inside the box. "I'm sorry we didn't trust you. It's just that, well, after what happened…"

"I know." Therese climbed to her feet.

Richard returned the lid to the box and handed it over. The two of them hugged her, asked again if she was okay, and, after she told them she was, left her alone with her pets and the box.

She returned the box to her dresser, wondering now if it was all over. She had failed to deliver it to Persephone without opening it. Technically, she hadn't opened it. Her uncle had. Did that count?

She asked Than to send her a message. What was she supposed to do?

She looked up from the box to her reflection in the mirror over her dresser. The red-haired twins had called her ugly and plain. She knew she wasn't beautiful, but was she ugly? She studied her features and thought they'd been right. Why had Than chosen her, of all the girls in the world? She was the first to ever kiss him. Was he sure he loved her? Would he always love her? For all eternity? Or would he grow tired of her plain looks?

Maybe she should take a bit of the beauty from the ring. Just a little, so Than wouldn't spend eternity regretting his decision. She could still return the ring to the box. It had already been opened. It had already been touched by her aunt. Who would know if Therese slipped it on her finger?

She put her hand on the lid, her fingers tingling. No. There was still a chance she hadn't failed. She pulled her hand away and flung herself on her bed.

Throughout the day, Therese searched for signs of what she should do with the box, continually praying to Persephone, Aphrodite, and Than, to the point she worried she was either annoying them or had already failed and no god wanted to speak to her again. She sat on her bed with her laptop and researched the five challenges. She read the story about Cupid and Psyche. Aphrodite tested Psyche with the black box of beauty, and Psyche failed.

She researched the golden apples of the Hesperides. Hera was given the orchard as a wedding gift. They were her apples. Maybe

Therese could find a way to get a golden apple without having to fight the dragon. Hmm.

It was a relief to leave after lunch, after hiding the box in the bottom drawer of her dresser beneath several pairs of sweats, to groom Stormy at the Holts.

That is, until Pete came into the barn.

He sauntered up to her with a confident smile and took her in his arms. "Afternoon, good-lookin'," he said with his chin on the top of her head. He released her and pecked her nose. "I sure enjoyed last night."

"Me, too." She plucked Stormy's brush from a shelf, trying to keep her hands from shaking. "Isn't Jen coming?"

"I told her I'd groom Sassy today. Hope that's okay." It was Sunday, which meant no trail rides. He stepped to the back of the stall to avoid getting between Stormy and Sassy.

"Sure. I just thought she might want to talk, that's all." Therese sat on a stool at the front of the stall and held the brush out for Stormy to inspect. Then she gently rubbed Stormy's withers. Stormy didn't need to be groomed at such a young age, but the Holts wanted him trained and used to people before he was weaned. "She told me how hard it's been on her with your dad..."

Pete's voice was low and strained when he said, "Let's not talk about that right now."

"I'm sorry."

They brushed in the silence for a while, and then Pete asked, "So how about a movie sometime this week? We could go to dinner, too, if you want."

Therese closed her eyes and took a deep breath.

"You don't seem enthusiastic," Pete said, standing over her.

She looked up at him from her stool, unaware till that moment he could see her face. She opened her mouth to speak, but nothing came out.

"A change of heart already?" he asked softly. He took her hand and lifted her to him, searching her eyes.

The last thing she wanted to do was hurt him. Her stomach clenched into a tight knot and the rest of her body went numb. His eyes were full of hurt. "Pete, I…"

He kissed her, and though she accepted the first gentle kiss, she pulled her lips away. "I'm sorry. I'm confused, Pete. I still have feelings for Than."

He closed his eyes and sighed. Then he squeezed her hand and said, "Let me know when you're over him."

She stood there as he put away Sassy's brush and left the barn with his head down.

After dinner, Therese sat on her bed with Clifford and stared at the little black box on her dresser. Could her chances with Than really be over so soon, on the very first challenge? If Hades cared at all about justice, then no. For the first time since her failure last summer on Mount Olympus, she directed a prayer to Hades. She stood up, stared fiercely at her reflection over the dresser, and said in a low, angry voice, "I have *not* failed. I have *not* failed. Send me to Persephone, so I can deliver the box."

She waited. Nothing happened.

She put her hands to her head and pulled her hair. "Then I'm going to Mount Olympus to look for her myself!" It was summer. Persephone should be with her mother, Demeter. Than told her that in fall and winter, when Persephone returned to the Underworld, Demeter left Mount Olympus and shut herself up in a winter cottage on Mount Parnassus. But in spring and summer, both goddesses lived on Mount Olympus.

Therese took the traveling robe from her closet and slipped her arms through each sleeve. Picking up the box, she imagined herself in the middle of the court, and before she could think twice about what she was doing, the invisible plastic wrapped around her, and she was god traveling.

She closed her eyes, afraid to discover where she had landed, when her feet hit solid ground, and afraid to look upon the gods without warning. Last summer, they had protected her from their brightness, but would they today, after she barged into the palace uninvited?

In her mind, she prayed, "Please accept me, please accept me, please accept me."

"Open your eyes, Therese," came a woman's soft voice.

Therese peeked through one half-closed lid to find Persephone before her, her hands on the box.

"Thank you for delivering the box to me. You have completed your first challenge."

Therese opened her other eye and looked around the court. Not all the gods were present today. The virgin goddesses—Athena, Artemis, and Hestia—were absent, as were all the gods save Zeus and Hephaestus. The latter now approached her carrying a sword and shield. Her sword and shield.

"Much luck to you," Hephaestus said, handing them to her. "And congratulations for getting this far."

Therese accepted the weapon and shield from Hephaestus and thanked him with a bow.

His misshapen face crinkled into a grin full of deep lines and hanging flesh, reminding Therese of a French bulldog. Now that she had a good look at him, he didn't seem ugly. He wasn't beautiful, but he wasn't ugly either. He had character. "If there's anything more I can do to help, please let me know," he said.

"Thank you, sir. But I'm not allowed to accept help with the five challenges."

"But you can accept advice."

Therese glanced around the palace courtroom where only a few goddesses remained talking among themselves. No one paid attention to her and Hephaestus. "Yes. Yes, I can."

"So how can I help?"

"Can you tell me how I might get Hera to like me?"

"I'm afraid not. She's my mother, but she has no love for me because I'm ugly."

Therese frowned. "Sir, you're not ugly to me."

He gave her another crinkly smile.

She bowed to him once again and turned toward Hera, her heart picking up speed and pulsing in her throat. She wasn't sure yet what she was going to say, but she had to try something. A hundred heads were too many for anyone, except maybe Hercules, even with the crown of invisibility.

In her mind, she prayed to Hera, "May I approach you?"

Hera turned to her and bid her forward to her throne, Zeus's side still unoccupied. A lucky break, Therese thought.

"What do you ask of me?" Hera said.

Therese had trouble forming a thought much less a string of words. She bowed her head and said, "Hades has given me a set of challenges."

"I'm aware of what goes on in this court."

Okay, not a good start. "I don't want to offend you by taking a golden apple from your orchard without your permission."

"Permission granted, so long as you don't eat the apple. Return it to Mount Olympus intact."

"Could you give it to me, madam? I would be happy to serve you."

"You would serve me even without the favor."

Oh, no. Therese just did what she'd hoped to avoid. She had offended Hera. "Yes, madam."

"Then bring me a fan made of peacock feathers when you deliver the golden apple."

Therese nodded and bowed. "How will I get past the one-hundred-headed dragon?"

"A bit of cake laced with sleeping pills will put Ladon to sleep, but he's not your problem. The Hesperides won't fall for that trick."

She'd read online the Hesperides were three nymphs, daughters of Atlas, but she found nothing more about them. "How can I convince them to let me take an apple?"

"Distract them with your flute. Now leave me. I've other matters to attend to."

Therese meant to ask where Hera's garden was located, but she didn't dare delay the goddess.

Chapter Twenty-One: Than's Objection

Than had hovered above Therese's house watching the sons of Aphrodite and Ares, Fear and Panic, taunt Therese as she held the little black box. He shouldn't have been surprised by her resistance to their powers. Her strong will had amazed him from the beginning. But when the twin gods had finally vanished and Therese had looked at her reflection with new doubts about her beauty, he wanted to kill the boy lions with his bare hands.

He rushed to his father's chambers to object, his heart pumping fast and loud, like it might burst from his chest. Hades sat at a golden table with Tizzie and Meg, apparently arguing. They all three looked up as Than approached, unable to hide his anger.

"Ares had no right!" Than spat the words out as he crossed the room. "You said no gods could intervene."

"I said help," Hades corrected. "I said no god may help her."

"And I thought you were the god of justice!"

"These are challenges, Thanatos. The more challenging, the better the victory."

"Hah! Admit it. You want her to fail!"

Hades didn't hide the smile creeping across his face as he stood and met Than's eyes, their noses inches apart. "I want her to pay! She was an embarrassment to me last summer. If she's to join us here in my palace, I want her to suffer first."

"The punishment should fit the crime!" Than said.

"Agreed!" Hades bellowed. "I said those very words to your sisters before you arrived. They want to drag on too long the punishment of a murderer in Paris before they bring him here. I think they are motivated by something other than justice."

The Furies stood up, their eyes changing from blue in one and brown in the other to dark red. Blood dripped to their cheeks.

"Who doesn't love Paris?" Tizzie hissed.

"We'll leave you now," Meg snarled.

The Furies vanished.

Hades crossed his arms at his chest. "And you are, too, Thanatos."

"She had compassion for a man who was no longer a threat to her. She refused to kill him in cold blood. How is that a failure?"

"He deserved death. Her parents deserved vengeance. You deserved her to keep her word! She's the one who let you down, son. Not me. She chose to have mercy on that killer over becoming your wife. Doesn't that bother you even a little?"

Than's throat tightened and no words came. He could think of nothing to say. Yes, it had bothered him. It had bothered him a lot. Only her prayers in the aftermath of the battle convinced him of her love. Her prayers, not her actions.

The challenges gave her the opportunity to remedy that. His father was right.

Chapter Twenty-Two: The Golden Apple

Back in her room in Colorado, relieved she succeeded in her first challenge, Therese searched the internet for more information about Hera's golden apple orchard. She sat on her bed with her laptop across her legs and Clifford curled up beside her. Most websites placed the orchard in the Atlas Mountains of Morocco in Northwest Africa. One website described a fabled orchard in Marrakesh on the edge of the Majorelle Garden.

Therese wondered why it was called a *fabled* garden. If Hades wanted her to pluck an apple and bring it to Mount Olympus, the garden must exist, but wouldn't at least one website verify that? The only logical explanation for the lack of information about the orchard was that it must be invisible to mortals, and if it was invisible, how would Therese be able to find it?

Gods weren't supposed to help her face the challenges, but they could advise her, as Hephaestus pointed out. Therese closed her laptop, knelt on the floor, and pulled her flute case and music stand from beneath her bed. She played a new ballad she learned her sophomore year as a tribute to Hermes, and as her fingers slipped over the cool metal keys of the instrument, she prayed for his advice.

Not long into the ballad, Hermes appeared in the chair beneath her window, playing his pipe in harmony with her flute. The effect was so beautiful that tears welled in her eyes. She couldn't believe she was contributing to such a perfect sound, the smooth notes reaching high in a trill, only to go low, slow, and long. Her fingers trembled; she didn't want to ruin the beautiful song with a wrong note. When the song finally ended unmarred by her, Therese smiled with both relief and gratitude across the room at the messenger god. "Thank you."

"My pleasure," Hermes said, without getting up. "To answer your question: To see Hera's apple orchard, wear the crown from Artemis. Only when you're invisible to mortal eyes will you be able to see what mortals cannot see."

Before Therese could ask another question, or thank him for his advice, Hermes disappeared.

Hermes's advice reminded Therese of a fact she'd forgotten: Artemis's crown made her invisible to *mortal* eyes. The immortal beings could still see her. The crown might help her find the orchard, but it wouldn't protect her from being seen by the Hesperides or the one-hundred-headed dragon, not to mention the Minotaur and the Hydra. She'd been counting on the advantage of invisibility. Even if she were successful in the second challenge, what chance did she have against the two monsters if they could see her?

Therese slumped on her bed, twisting her bedcovers in her hands. This was crazy. She would die. Last summer at Mount Olympus, she was ready to die. She longed for her parents and knew her aunt would be protected by Ares, as part of their deal in her accepting the choice to fight McAdams. But now that she better understood what a life at Than's side would mean, she wanted to live. She didn't want to be like her parents in the Underworld, without free will, without personality, and without much knowledge of the existence of others. She wanted to live.

Though after what happened with Vicki, she would rather die than face her friends when it was time to go back to school. If she could live with Than, she could escape those judging eyes. Poor Vicki. Maybe she could do something for her once she was a god.

But making it through the challenges seemed impossible to her now. Than was right when he said the challenges were designed to punish her. Maybe she shouldn't have accepted them so hastily. Maybe she should have allowed Than to take her directly to Demeter's winter cottage and turn her himself, even though it meant torture forever for him. At least they'd be together.

No. She couldn't stand the thought of him being ripped to pieces every year. Her death was better than his torture. She had to try.

And it was too late to turn back now. She'd already accepted the challenges, and she'd completed the first of them. There was nothing to do but to keep going.

Monday morning, Therese went, for the first time since Vicki's funeral, to swim practice with Jen at the city natatorium, their high school pool still under repair from the earthquake damage. As Jen drove them home afterward, Therese brought up the crown.

"I'll have it back to you tonight," Therese promised, though she worried she might not be able to keep it.

Jen looked at her like a wilted flower, quavering in the wind. She nodded and returned her eyes to the road. Before dropping off Therese, she drove to her own house and got the crown.

"I'll come by later." Therese climbed from the pickup with the crown hidden beneath her towel.

After eating a burger Richard had picked up in town, Therese sat on the living room sofa beside Carol, who had her laptop resting on the coffee table where she worked her pharmaceutical sales. Sometimes Carol had to travel out of town, but she was never gone for more than a few days at a time.

"Everything okay?" Carol asked.

Therese shrugged. She couldn't say how wrong it seemed that she had lived and Vicki had died. She also couldn't tell how she was about to put herself in danger and wanted to sit with Carol awhile in case it was the last time. She wanted to say, "I'm scared," but instead she said, "Yeah."

Carol put an arm around Therese's shoulders and they leaned back on the sofa. Therese crossed her ankles on the coffee table, something her parents allowed and used to do themselves. Carol closed her laptop and did the same.

"Maybe we should do something fun together this week," Carol said. "We could go rafting, or we could take the Silverton train. What sounds good to you?"

Therese shrugged again. "It doesn't matter to me. Whatever you want to do."

"I can take a break now if you want to watch a movie together."

Therese wanted to watch a movie. She wanted to sit quietly beside her aunt, her last remaining blood relative, and feel her close beside her once more before facing the immortal monsters. But if she wanted to start the first challenge today, she didn't have much time before it would be dark in Marrakesh. According to the web, there was a seven hour time difference between Colorado and Morocco. "How about tonight, after supper?" Hopefully, she'd be alive and back by then.

"Okay, sweetheart."

"I'm going to take a nap." Therese got up from the sofa and went upstairs, Clifford on her heels. She was ready to put on the traveling robe from Aphrodite.

The Majorelle Garden in Marrakesh, Morocco bustled with tourists weaving up and down floral-lined stone paths and over bridges across ponds of lily pads and through antique stone buildings full of paintings. Cobalt blue fountains, railings, and trim unified the otherwise multi-colored flowers and foliage. Therese sifted through the crowd and

135

found her way just outside the garden near the trails leading up the Atlas Mountains. A dozen tents and donkeys peppered the valley with the aromas of freshly cooked dinners wafting toward the sky. Picnic tables, scattered across the valley, held tourists eating the food these makeshift restaurants prepared beneath their tents. Therese's belly rumbled at the delicious smells even though back in Durango, she'd just eaten a burger and was full. It was lunchtime back home; here, it was seven in the evening.

She wondered what these people thought of her wearing the silk robe, the golden scabbard at her waist, and the golden shield on her back, carrying a flute in one hand and a crown in the other. Maybe they thought she was an entertainer. It occurred to Therese that, indeed, she was, for Hades.

She wore her purse strapped around her neck and hanging at one hip. It carried a cinnamon roll leftover from breakfast and stuffed with SleepAid caplets and the Prozac she never finished taking. Scouring the landscape for the perfect place to disappear, she trekked past the tents and picnic tables into a copse of pines leading up a mountain. Once she was in the thick of them, she placed the crown on her head as her heart sped up and her fingers twitched.

Immediately, the landscape changed. The pines disappeared, and in their place were fruit trees. She stood between a row of pear and another of orange. Taking a few hesitant steps, she saw no sign of the three nymphs or their dragon. With trembling hands, she put the flute to her bottom lip and played, telling herself that it would be okay if she died. She wouldn't know any better. The Lethe would wipe away her memories and infuse her with a pleasant feeling of contentment for all eternity.

When she reached the end of the rows, she froze. Her fingers would no longer move and all the air rushed out of her body, leaving her nothing to blow across the flute. Three beautiful ladies lounging on the thick, gnarly roots of a giant apple tree looked up at her with their mouths open in surprise and delight, but wrapped around the trunk of the tree was the body of the biggest snake Therese had ever seen, its many green heads looking at her from the branches, blending with the green leaves except for their yellow eyes and flicking tongues. Round, golden apples hung from the branches, but none were within arm's reach from the ground. The ladies all had long black braids and skin the same color of the ashy brown tree trunk. If it weren't for their soft cotton gowns of different colors billowing in the gentle breeze, they would have blended in with the trunk and roots of the tree. Their dark eyes narrowed at Therese suspiciously, so she took in air—though it burned—and blew. The ladies smiled at her again.

One of the three hopped to her feet and took the hand of her sister. Soon all three danced to Therese's melody. She was afraid to stop, playing and playing for hours until the sun began to set and her fingers felt raw and her throat tight. Worried she'd be too weak to fight if necessary, she stopped playing and decided to speak.

"Hello, Hesperides. My name is Therese. Hera gave me permission to pick an apple from her tree and take it to Mount Olympus."

The three ladies laughed, looking over their shoulder at Ladon's many heads glaring at Therese from the branches.

Therese opened her purse and took out the cinnamon roll. "Hera gave me a gift to give to Ladon." It wasn't exactly true. Technically, Hera hadn't given it to her. But it had been her idea. Too frightened to approach the tree and the nymphs, Therese tossed the roll through the air where it was caught and eaten by one of Ladon's hundred heads.

The middle and tallest nymph stepped toward Therese. "Why would Hera allow you to pick an apple and not one of us, who have been her servants for centuries?"

"She told me I wasn't to eat it, but to bring it to her."

This information made the nymph nod and reconsider Therese, but the other two dashed forward and took Therese by the arms.

"I want to keep her," one of them said.

"Me too," the other said.

Therese tried to pull free but couldn't loosen their hold on her.

"We're so bored," said one.

"We want you to stay and play for us."

Therese looked at the apple tree and noticed Ladon's hundred heads drooping from the branches, all two hundred eyes closed. She wasn't sure how long the drugs would work. She had to get away from the nymphs before the dragon awoke.

"I have an idea," Therese said. "I'll give you my flute and teach you to play if you let me take an apple from the tree while Ladon sleeps."

"He never sleeps."

The nymphs followed Therese's gaze to the tree, then turned to her with ravenous smiles.

"Ha!"

The three rushed to the tree and took several apples each, biting into them with pleasure, moaning and squealing with delight. Therese thought of grabbing one for herself and making a run for it, but she was afraid the nymphs could outrun her, and three to one were difficult odds to overcome. But she had a sword and they were unarmed.

But they were nymphs and had special powers.

Then she remembered her silver robe. She'd used it to travel from her home in Colorado to the Majorelle Garden in Marrakesh. She'd never used it to travel a few yards at a time. Could she be that precise with god travel? She could dart to one of the upper branches, grab an apple, and then return to her bedroom. She decided to try.

She focused on a thick branch out of the reach of the nymphs. The invisible plastic wrapped around her, and she landed, precariously

138

perched next to one of Ladon's heads. She lifted one leg in the air and leaned forward to maintain her balance and plucked an apple just as one of the nymphs screamed.

Ladon had awakened and had wrapped a neck around each of the nymphs. The head next to Therese's foot opened its eyes and glared at her. She focused on her room in Colorado, but nothing happened. Why couldn't she god travel? She tried again, but the snake pulled back its head, about to strike.

Therese jumped from the high branch and fell to the ground, landing on her hands and knees, pain shooting through her legs and arms and back, the crown tossed to the ground beside her. She could no longer see the garden or the snake as she scrambled to her feet, but the invisible snake grabbed a hold of her legs and yanked her toward the invisible tree. The skin on her arms scraped against the ground. She focused again on her bedroom in Colorado. The invisible plastic wrapped itself around her and she fell to the floor in her room, the golden apple still clutched in her hand.

She did it! She got the apple! She jumped to her feet and looked at her victorious reflection in her dresser mirror.

Then she remembered the crown. What would Jen do without it? She had to go back! But how would she find the orchard without it? She wouldn't be able to see what's invisible to mortal eyes unless she wore the crown. Slumped on her bed, picturing Jen's face, she was overwhelmed by a blend of disappointment and terror. She had to find a way to protect her friend, especially since she hadn't been able to protect Vicki.

The next morning, Jen called to say she wasn't going to swim practice; Therese would have to find another ride.

Therese's eyes squeezed closed as she clutched the phone to her ear. "Are you sick?"

"Sort of."

"What do you mean?"

"Why didn't you call last night? I didn't sleep a wink."

"Did your Dad…"

"No. I stayed in the barn with Stormy and Sassy."

"Jen, I'm…"

"It's not your fault. I'm sorry. It's not your fault I live with a pig."

"Stay with me tonight."

"Can I? That'd be great. Can I have the crown back?"

Therese couldn't think of what to say.

"Therese?"

"Yes. Of course you can."

That afternoon, after a trip with Carol to the craft store in Durango, Therese sat on the wooden floor of her room constructing a fan out of peacock feathers using a hot glue gun. The eight fluffy feathers were long and beautiful. She used the glue to attach them at the base. Then she wound blue yarn tightly around the bottom, gluing it in place, making a handle. She hoped Hera would be pleased. As she cleaned up, she prayed to the gods to inspire her to think of a way to get back the crown. She was surprised when Artemis appeared before her, the crown in her hand.

"The apple for the crown," Artemis said sternly.

"What?"

"You heard me."

"But I told Hera I would deliver the apple to her at Mount Olympus."

140

"Then I'll keep the crown."

"Wait!" Therese couldn't leave Jen without protection.

"Will it still count? My challenge, I mean? If I give you the apple, will it still count as a victory?"

"You're to deliver an apple to Mount Olympus."

"So that's a no?"

Artemis frowned with impatience.

Therese opened her dresser drawer, found the apple, and handed it over to Artemis.

Artemis gave her the crown and vanished.

Great, Therese thought. She was back at square one. Not wanting to waste any more time, she put her arms through the silver robe and strapped her sword and shield to her body. She doubted the cake of sleeping pills would work a second time, plus she had used all but one of the SleepAid caplets and all of her Prozac. But she had a plan. She would put on the crown and god travel directly to one of the branches of the tree, pick an apple, and disappear before Ladon could react. Now that she'd seen the tree, she should be able to go directly to it.

Just as she was about to god travel, she heard Carol calling up the stairs. "I'm making milkshakes, sweetheart. Want one?"

Therese grinned. Milkshake or dangerous mission to North Africa? Hmm. Tough choice. Then she decided she'd have both. "Sure. I'll be down in a minute." Might as well be an optimist.

She closed her eyes, focused on the golden apple tree, and...nothing. She blinked at her reflection in her dresser mirror. She recalled how she'd been unable to travel from the branch to her bedroom. Maybe something about the tree interfered? She closed her eyes and imagined the orchard. Nothing. Maybe it was the crown. She hadn't made it back to Colorado until the crown had fallen from her head.

141

She took the crown in one hand, closed her eyes, and focused again on the tree, and was instantly surrounded by invisible plastic. When she opened her eyes, she was standing in the copse of pines on the outskirts of Majorelle Garden.

This must mean she couldn't travel between visible and invisible locations.

She placed the crown on her head and saw the orchard surrounding her. She focused on the treetop and opened her eyes as soon as she felt her foot hit the branch.

One of Ladon's necks wrapped around her ankle as another prepared to strike. Therese pulled out her sword and sliced off the striking head, grabbed an apple, and cut her ankle free. She god traveled to the middle of the orchard, but the snake's long body lurched out at her with at least ten of its heads. Her heart pounded in her ears as she fell to the ground, nearly losing the crown as it slipped from her hair. She grabbed the crown with two fingers from the hand holding the sword, nearly cutting off her ear as she fell among the pines, focusing on her bedroom. The invisible plastic closed around her, and when it released her, she found herself sprawled on all fours on her bed, her sword sticking straight up from her mattress like Excalibur from its rock.

Her mattress might be ruined, and her right ear was bleeding, but at least she had the apple *and* the crown! She jumped from her bed, never happier, and lifted Clifford into her arms. He barked and wagged his tail excitedly.

It was time to go downstairs and have that milkshake.

Chapter Twenty-Three: Godliness

Than came to Mount Olympus more often in the past year than he had his entire life, and it seemed the other gods were less wary of his presence, which was good. He felt less disconnected from the rest of his kind. He had Therese to thank for that.

He avoided Hera's hard, cold gaze and did not look forward to her treatment of Therese when Therese arrived with the golden apple. Hera was not pleased by the gorging on her fruit by the Hesperides or by the injuries to her pet dragon, but worse was the fact that Artemis possessed one of her precious apples. The garden was a wedding present from Gaia to Hera when she married Zeus. The apples were precious to Hera, and she was stingy with them. They'd only been touched by others a few times, and the one stolen by Eris had been the start of the Trojan War. Eris had thrown the apple into the company of gods and goddesses with a note attached, "For the most beautiful," and three goddesses—Athena, Aphrodite, and Hera—had each claimed the apple belonged to her. They agreed to let a mortal named Paris choose. Hera was not chosen, though secretly Than believed she should have been. He wondered what Artemis planned to do with her apple.

Than knew Ares had just left the city of Paris for Mount Olympus and had timed his own arrival with that of the other god's. After a rendezvous with Aphrodite, Ares might be in a good mood. Than spoke with his mother and grandmother briefly then turned to the god of war, the only god present except for Zeus and Hephaestus.

Ares recoiled in surprise. "What could you possibly want from me, Cousin?"

"It's what you want, Ares."

"I'm listening."

"Which would you enjoy more: a quick slaughter or a more evenly matched battle?"

"You know the answer."

"Then join me tonight in the dream world to give Therese some advice on how best to face the Minotaur. She has no experience with her sword."

"Last summer was a disappointment."

"She'll die at the Minotaur's hands, but with your tips, she may delay her death and entertain you." And give me time to save her, Than thought.

"Tonight then."

Before Than turned to leave, he sensed Therese's presence. All of the gods toned down their brightness to prepare for mortal eyes, and in a split second, Therese appeared before Hera bearing a golden apple and a fan of peacock feathers.

Hera's raging voice made Therese fall to her knees. She set the apple and fan at the goddess's feet.

"What will Artemis do with my apple?" Hera screeched.

"I don't know," Therese said meekly, her eyes to the marble floor. "But it was the only way I could protect my friend. You're the goddess of marriage and children. Surely you understand my friend's need of the crown."

"You shouldn't have dropped it in the first place."

Than was about to speak on Therese's behalf when Zeus beat him to it. "She's only human, dear. Don't be so harsh. I'm pleased she's made it this far."

Therese dipped her head, and climbed to her feet. As she turned to leave, she met Than's eyes and rushed to his side.

"I'll come to you tonight, in your dreams." He touched her lips with his and then left the palace before his presence made her weak. He hovered above to watch her from a safe distance.

He was surprised to see her walk across the palace floor to Hephaestus.

"I thought you might feel better knowing Hera doesn't like me either," she said.

"Not to worry," Hephaestus said with a crinkly smile. "Whoever is cursed by Hera is automatically protected by Zeus. You now have the special protection of the king of the gods."

At that moment, Than vowed to himself to help his cousin whenever it was in his power to do so.

Hades had given Than permission to change places with Hip once more because he'd been pleased by Therese's performance. Hip refused to trade until Therese was asleep, wanting to hold off the odious duties of death for as long as possible. So now, Than hovered above her house, waiting.

His heart lightened as he listened in on Therese's conversation with Jen. The two girls lay side by side on the bed with Clifford between them, their heads turned close, their voices low. Jen told stories about her horses, her brother Bobby, and a classmate they both disliked. Therese warmed him with her musical laugh, running her fingers over a hole in the middle of the mattress. He couldn't wait to hold her.

When the girls finally turned off the bedside lamp and said their goodnights, Than met Hip at the field of poppies and entered the world of dreams.

Chapter Twenty-Four: Ares

Therese fell on her knees in a dark alley, the pavement scraping her skin. She climbed to her feet and glanced in all directions. Tall buildings and garbage cans flanked the alley, along with a few cars, but Therese saw no sign of people, no sign of life at all, not even a stray cat or dog.

She was barefoot and wearing her nightshirt, which meant she was dreaming. Before she could kick off the ground and swim through the air to test this theory, someone grabbed her from behind, an arm wrenched around her neck. She couldn't break away.

"You know what they say is true don't you?" a gruff but familiar voice murmured at her ear. "If you die in your dream, you die for real."

The mention of the word dream reminded her that she could do what she wanted. She elbowed the man and god traveled away from him. Who needed a traveling robe in the dream world? She placed herself in her grandparents' old house in San Antonio, not sure why she ended up there so often. Maybe it was a place of comfort. Maybe it was because she associated the place with family. She shook her head. Why am I analyzing my dream now, while I'm still in the middle of it? This is crazy. She willed her grandparents on the living room couch, with Blue, their Blue Merle Australian Shepherd, on the green carpet at their feet.

She sensed a presence outside the front door. A quarter-inch gap appeared around the door, through which bright, ominous light spilled in. Therese pushed her full weight against the door, to keep whatever wanted in out, but the door dissolved and she fell against the hard chest of Ares, god of war.

This is a dream, this is a dream, she repeated beneath her breath, as she stumbled back. "Figment, I command you to show yourself!"

"I'm no figment, Therese."

Therese god traveled from her grandparents' house to the wooden deck in Colorado.

I'm going to make this a happy dream, she said to herself. She willed a chipmunk to appear on the railing beside her.

"Come here, little fella."

The chipmunk hopped onto her hand and let her pet him. She fed him a handful of seeds. Then she thought of Puffy, and turned the chipmunk into him. "Puffy! I miss you so much!" She pressed his soft, furry face against her cheek.

Ares appeared at her side wearing a wry smile. "I see why Hypnos and Thanatos admire you. But this won't help you defeat the Minotaur."

"Why do you care?" Shut up, Therese thought.

Ares laughed.

Than appeared at her side.

"Than? Is that really you?" She wondered if she should repeat her command for figments. She threw her arms around him instead, needing him, even if it was just a stupid figment. She'd take him any way she could get him.

He cupped her face and showered her with kisses, pressing his warm lips to her eyelids, her nose, her cheeks, her forehead, and her mouth. It felt so real. If only she could make Ares disappear. "Make him disappear," she prayed to Than with her eyes closed.

"He's here to help you."

She opened her eyes. "What? Why?"

"Can we please get started?" Ares said impatiently. "I don't have all night."

"He's agreed to teach you how to fight."

"He killed my parents! I don't want his help!"

147

Her scabbard and shield appeared strapped to her body, startling her.

Than kissed her once more. "Do this for me."

Therese's heart thudded in her ears. She couldn't believe Than was asking her to work with Ares. Her hands shook—out of anger, not fear, and hatred.

"When you face the Minotaur, have your sword drawn," Ares said, drawing his own. "If you wait, you'll be at a disadvantage. Carry it out in the ready position as you make your way through the labyrinth."

Therese drew her sword, narrowing her eyes at him. She wanted to slice off his head.

Ares faced her. "Spread your feet. Wider. You'll lose your balance otherwise. Keep them spread as you walk."

Therese did as he said.

"Bend your knees and lean forward, like this."

She copied his stance.

"Hold the sword closer to your body. If you hold it too far out like this, you make yourself vulnerable to attack. There."

Therese couldn't believe the god of war was being nice to her, and without realizing it, she said the question in the form of a prayer to him. "Why are you being so nice to me?"

He looked down at her, his hand still on hers, adjusting the position of her sword to her body. "I just want to see a good fight."

She lowered her eyes, the blood rushing to her face. She wanted to kill him.

"Keep your elbows in," he said, stepping back from her. "Remember, you want to use the sword, not your arms. If your arm goes out like this, it's easy to get it lobbed off. Repeat to yourself, elbows in. By instinct, you'll want to keep your body as far away as possible from your opponent, forcing you to reach out with your arms, but don't. It's

148

better to get closer, elbows in, so the sword can protect you on your sword side while your shield protects the other. Now, take the shield."

She did as he said.

Ares transformed into a giant beast with the body of a man and the head of a bull. It charged her. She backed away.

"Stay perpendicular to me," Ares's voice shouted through the beast's ferocious mouth. "With your shield side toward me."

She clenched her teeth, accidentally biting hard on her tongue. What had she been thinking when she agreed to fight the Minotaur?

"Feet apart, Therese. Crouch. You want to lower your center of gravity, or he'll knock you right over."

It had been a moment of insanity, she thought, crouching.

"Shift back and forth on your feet. Keep your mind clear. Anticipate my every move."

He lunged for her, and the only thing she could think to do was to will him into a butterfly.

He fluttered his yellow wings twice, a two-inch creature just above her head, before resuming his form as the god of war in front of her. "I'm impressed. But you won't be able to do that when you face the real Minotaur."

She glanced over at Than, the corners of his mouth turned down. "How am I going to do this?" she prayed.

He didn't reply.

Chapter Twenty-Five: A Labyrinthine Dream

Go straight and down, not right or left, Therese reminded herself as she stepped into her silver robe and strapped on her gear. In her purse, beside a ball of yellow yarn, nestled four cinnamon rolls leftover from that morning's breakfast and wrapped in paper towels—two for Ariadne and two for the Minotaur. Therese had baked them for today's purposes. Plus, she knew they were Jen's favorites.

Inside the rolls were crushed sleeping pills Jen had brought the night before, as a favor to Therese, who said she hadn't been sleeping well since Vicki's death, which, although true, wasn't why she wanted them; she needed them for her third challenge. Once she'd realized the crown wouldn't work on immortal beings, she came up with plan B: drug her adversaries. This seemed like her best strategy, since she had little experience with the sword—though her success in defeating Ladon had given her a little more confidence, as had her lessons with Ares.

She closed her eyes and imagined the ancient city of Knossos on the island of Crete, based on photos she viewed on the web. The palace ruins stretched for acres and acres, so she focused on a group of trees between the "Little Palace" and the "Great Palace." The invisible plastic wrapped around her, and moments later she emerged beneath a tree beside a bench where two older ladies sat picnicking. They blinked at her. She gave them a friendly wave.

The two ladies looked at one another over their half-eaten sandwiches and then stared, wide-eyed, back at Therese.

"I was in the tree," Therese said, pointing up awkwardly.

The ladies smiled and nodded, as if to say, "Of course." Therese wondered what they thought of her robe, scabbard, and shield. At least she wasn't carrying her flute and crown, though she did have a headlight clipped to her sun-visor. She waved once more, turned from the ladies, and headed toward the Great Palace.

The last bus back to the modern city of Heraklion would leave in ten minutes, and until then, Therese wandered the grounds, waiting to face the Minotaur alone.

Last night's dream was a whirlwind of a memory to her now, but bits and pieces of her fighting Ares as the Minotaur throughout the night came back to her as she walked through the ruins. Although her favorite part of the dream had been after Ares had left, when she and Than spent the rest of the night together in his rooms, she had to admit fighting Ares had given her a thrill. The adrenaline rush had been incredible.

She followed the steps up to the North Entrance and Pillar Hall, the sunset coating the clouds in a backdrop of pink, purple, and orange. Other tourists ambled along the same path as Therese, but in the opposite direction, down toward the buses and cabs. When she reached the Pillar Hall, she was surprised by the fresco painting of a bull. It was larger than life in deep browns and blacks against the white stone. Two huge horns curled and pointed from each side of its ferocious head.

Did it resemble the Minotaur?

Seeing the image of the bull brought another wave of fear to Therese, so she reminded herself that she had to fight to save Than from an eternity of torment. She had no choice. She couldn't accept his hand otherwise. As Therese watched the last of the tourists taking their photos of the sunset, her thoughts and prayers went to Than. "I can do this," she said over and over in her mind. Then, a half hour later, when dusk had fully settled and the grounds were empty except for her, she said it out loud: "I can do this."

She followed the path past partially fallen stones into the large central court, searching for the Grand Staircase, hoping beyond hope the

151

drugged rolls would work. It would be hard for her to slay the Minotaur as he lay sleeping, because she didn't like taking life, any life, but knowing he was immortal and would come back made Therese think she could follow through with it, unlike last summer with McAdams. Uncertainty and doubt pricked at the back of her neck, with questions like, What if he refused the rolls? What if she had to actually fight him? Through the course of her dream, she'd improved with Ares, but the training had all been mental: her physical body had undergone none of it.

To the south of the central court, she found the stairs—refurbished, reinforced, and beautiful. Therese imagined the ancient civilization that once inhabited these walls. A shudder moved through her as she reached the bottom of the Grand Staircase, anticipating a raven-haired goddess to lead her to the ancient entrance. She drew her sword, as Ares had advised, so she was ready for any surprises. With her other hand, she took out the four cinnamon rolls and laid them by the fallen pillar Than had said marked the entrance. Her hands shook like a starving beggar, and she was suddenly sick. This could be it. Her death. The end of everything.

She took up her shield and waited, sweat forming on her forehead. She chewed on the inside of her mouth. "I can do this," she said again.

A dark-haired woman appeared. *Woman* was hardly the word. She looked the same age as Therese. Her black wavy hair hung over her shoulders and across a white cotton dress that stopped below the knee. She was barefoot and frowning.

"Who are you?"

"Therese. Hades sent me. I brought cinnamon cakes." Therese tried to keep the tremor from her voice and the quake from her hand as she pointed her sword to the four rolls.

"Why should I trust you when you stand there prepared to kill me?"

Oh, no. Therese sucked in air. What should she do? Ares said to keep the sword in the ready position, but Ariadne wouldn't eat the cakes as long as it was drawn. If she did put the sword away, the Minotaur could sweep down on her out of nowhere, and it would all be over, just like that. Therese returned the sword to its scabbard.

Ariadne picked up one of the rolls. "It smells delicious. You have one first."

This was not going well at all. Now what should she do? She prayed to Than and Ares, like that would do any good. Than couldn't come near her without killing her himself, and Ares *wanted* her dead. She took the roll. "I baked these for you, Ariadne, and for your brother, Asterion."

Ariadne's eyes lit up. "You're the first to come here and call him by his rightful name. Most only know him as the Minotaur."

"It's not his fault he's what he is," Therese said.

The Minotaur appeared at Ariadne's side. "You seem friendly," he said, "and yet you arrived ready to attack."

"To defend," Therese said. "I just want to negotiate through the labyrinth and prove to Hades I can do it. I don't want to fight you."

"Very well," he said, though she didn't quite trust him. "I'll take your cakes in exchange for your entrance."

"Wait," Ariadne said. "Make her eat one first. They might be poisoned."

Therese put the roll to her lips and took a bite, trying to appear more confident than she was. Maybe a small bite wouldn't affect her. "It's delicious." She said. "Please, have one."

Ariadne took one and gave the other two to her brother. They watched her, waiting for her to take another bite, so she did. Together, the three of them ate the rolls. Therese began to feel sleepy.

"May I enter?" She hoped she wouldn't fall asleep before making it back out. She had no idea how long the maze was, but she needed to get started right away, though now she realized she would likely fall asleep in the middle of it and never escape alive.

"Yes," the Minotaur said, sitting down on a stone ledge. "We'll wait for you here. I think I'll take a nap."

Ariadne narrowed her eyes at Therese. "You wicked girl! You tricked us! You put something in the cakes to make us sleepy!" Ariadne sat on the ledge, fighting sleep.

"I'm sorry!" Therese cried. "I was afraid I couldn't trust you. I'm so sorry!" Therese staggered under the weight of her heavy shield and fell to the ground. She laid her head on her folded arms and went to sleep on the cold stone path, her last thought that the Minotaur would kill her.

Therese ran down a brightly lit hall, someone just ahead of her out of reach. Where was she? Shops lined the empty, narrow corridor that twisted and turned around vendor stands with handbags, toys, cell phones, and other products, creating a maze. She was inside a mall.

"Hey! Stop!" Therese turned a corner. Wait a minute, she thought, slowing down. Who am I chasing? And why? She rested her palms on her knees and caught her breath.

Hip appeared before her. "This is important. If you die in your dream, you die for real."

"Why are you telling me what I already know?"

They both turned their heads toward the sound of slow, heavy footsteps striking the tile floor. Twenty feet away, in front of The Gap, stood the Minotaur.

Hip moved closer to her. "I can't help you fight him, but if you kill him here in the dream world, you won't have to face him in the Upperworld."

"You mean that's not a figment? That's really him?"

"It's him alright."

"He looks mad."

"Yep. He's definitely mad." Hip put a hand on her shoulder. "You of all people have a chance of succeeding. Use your power to kill him here, in the dream world."

"Power?" Therese looked back at Hip to find him gone.

The Minotaur strolled boldly toward her. "That was a mean trick."

"Please forgive me, Asterion. I didn't think you'd let me traipse through your home and come out alive. All the stories paint you as a vicious killer. Can you blame me?"

"Yes. As a matter of fact, I can. People would be better off if they ignored rumors and sought the truth for themselves before passing judgment."

Therese took a step back with feet she could no longer feel as he moved closer. Her heart picked up speed, and she bit the inside of her mouth as she had this revelation: if I don't kill him here, in this dream, he will kill me when he wakes. I've got to kill him before he kills me. I have no choice. She braced herself as he bent his horns toward her and prepared to charge.

She turned him into a white rabbit, the kind magicians pull from black top hats, but he immediately returned to his tall, massive form, his eyes a little more fierce. She thought of running away—this was a mall, a labyrinth of another kind—but knew the longer she put off the inevitable, the more likely she would wake and find her chances gone.

In her mind, she said to him, I'm going to kill you.

He snarled with a grimace. "You're just a little girl."

His words inspired her to take charge of the dream again. She willed herself into a warrior, modeled after Athena, and then drew her sword. Rather than strike forward, which would make her arm vulnerable, she used a maneuver Ares had shown her: she twirled around, picked up momentum, lifted her arm as she came around, and struck the beast's side.

Although the blade wounded him, blood spilling across his ribs, he did not fall. He lunged at her. She shoved out her shield, her body perpendicular to him, as Ares had shown her, but the sheer force of his weight pushed her back, and she fell on the ground. When he lunged for her again, she turned herself into a snake and slithered between his legs to the back of him, returning to warrior form before he turned around. She took her sword and struck him at the neck, slicing through skin and fur, but again, he did not fall. He turned, and this time found her arm, and with terrifying strength pulled and flung her toward the ground.

Before she fell, she imagined herself as a rubbery, stretchy, malleable warrior, allowing her arm to be pulled past its natural length without causing her to tumble. She stretched her body out, like thick bubble gum, and wrapped herself tightly around him, but he pierced her with his horns, grabbed her arms, and tied them together before flinging her to his feet. She quickly untied her limbs, willed her sword and shield in place, but he caught on to her game and used his own will to manipulate the dream. He made his arm malleable and stretchy, maneuvered it past her sword and shield, and grabbed her by the neck, clutching his long fingers around her throat. Shocked, she looked at him, her mouth agape, unable to catch air. She tried to bring her sword across his arm, but, having learned from her, he bent it in all directions, easily missing her blade.

This is a dream, she reminded herself, and she turned herself into a puddle of water. She changed their landscape to that of a narrow cave, and she filled the cave with her water self, hoping to drown him. He solved the problem by becoming a shark.

I'm running out of time, she thought. We'll wake up, and I'll be screwed. She drained the cave of water in an instant, resuming her tall warrior form, and before the shark turned, brought down her sword. The shark flopped on the dry rocky ground of the cave, and for a moment, she thought she'd won, but before she could blink, the Minotaur was on his feet, ready to charge.

In that split second before he lunged for her, a number of options flew through her mind. She could make herself a bigger Minotaur than he, she could make herself Zeus and perhaps frighten him, or she could make herself fire and try burning him alive. But with each of these ideas came the thought of his counter: he could make himself bigger, he could make himself a Titan, or he could make himself water. At last, a new idea struck her, and before he reached her, she transformed into Ariadne, his sister, and said, "No, Asterion!"

The Minotaur stopped, bewildered, his bull mouth hanging open. Before he came to the realization that he was being tricked, Therese, still in Ariadne's form, drove her sword through the beast's chest, driving it all the way through to the back.

"Ariadne!" the Minotaur cried as he fell back to the rocky ground. He flailed his arms about, like a spider on its back. "You betrayed me. Again."

The real Ariadne must have heard him call out for her, for she appeared in the dream across from Therese, her double. Ariadne looked confused, apparently unaware that she was looking at Therese in disguise.

"What have I done?" Ariadne shrieked. "Oh, Asterion, look at me!" She dropped on her knees at his side. "Please forgive me!"

But her brother was already dead, his thick bull's tongue hanging from his sharp-teethed mouth.

Ariadne shrieked again, her hands on her brother's unmoving chest. Then she stood and pulled the blade from her brother's body. Therese thrust the shield forward, ready to defend herself, but gasped when, instead of attacking Therese, Ariadne drove the blade into her own heart and fell beside her brother.

Therese left the cave and stayed at her grandparents' house with Blue, pretending he wasn't a stupid figment, until the sleeping pills wore off and she awoke at the temple ruins in Knossos beside the dead bodies of the two immortal siblings. She put her hand to her mouth, unable to believe she had killed them. Why didn't she feel victorious, triumphant? Tears formed in her eyes and she clenched her teeth, accidentally cutting into the soft flesh of the tip of her tongue. To the fallen bodies, she whispered, "I'm sorry. I didn't want to do this."

She wasn't finished yet; she still had to make it through the labyrinth, and she had to do it before her victims—is that what they were, her victims?—revived. She pulled the ball of yellow yarn from her purse and unwound it, leaving a long strand at the entrance, and then, flipping on the headlight at her visor, plunged into the dark maze.

Chapter Twenty-Six: Therese's Prayers

Than laid a hand on the shoulders of each of the two siblings, Ariadne and Asterion, as he led their souls from the palace ruins in Knossos, Crete to the Underworld. Relieved and exhilarated by the success of Therese, who still laid sleeping at his feet, and wishing he could sneak a kiss on her cheek without endangering her life, Than made a stupid joke to the Minotaur, for which he was instantly sorry, something like, "At this rate, we'll have to get you a room of your own."

Asterion glared at Than and knocked the god of death's hand from his shoulder.

"Sorry, man. Bull. Bullman." Than inwardly cringed at his horrible lack of tact. He'd never felt so giddy. For the first time since his father issued the five challenges, he actually believed there was a chance—however slight—Therese would succeed. "Sorry. This way."

Not long after, he could hear her praying to him from the labyrinth. Her tone quickly changed from bewildered, "I can't believe I'm still alive," to regretful, "I can't believe I killed them." The more and more she expressed her sorrow over the souls he now helped board Charon's ferry, the less giddy he felt.

"Asterion and Ariadne would have let me through, I bet," Therese prayed. "I tricked them, angered them, and then killed them both. Ariadne may have held the sword, but I'm the one who drove her to use it. I don't want to be this person I'm becoming, Than. I don't want to kill the Hydra. Can't I win your father's approval without having to kill anything?"

He found it interesting that her new fear was not, "The Hydra will kill me," but "I must kill the Hydra and don't want to." Her victory over the Minotaur had given her confidence. Maybe too much.

He left the two immortal souls on the banks of the Lethe River in Erebus and then sought his father.

Than waited for nearly an hour in Hades's empty chamber, passing the time by listening to Therese's constant prayers to him, and was overjoyed to learn she'd navigated her way to safety. Not long after, Hades and Hermes appeared at the golden table, in mid conversation.

"It's a deal," Hermes said, shaking the other god's hand.

Once Hermes left Hades's table and father and son were alone, Than said, "I need clarification."

"Regarding?"

"When you said Therese must defeat the Hydra, did you mean 'kill' or 'overcome'?"

Hades stood from his golden table and crossed the room to his son. "What's this hair-splitting all about?"

"As you know, Therese succeeded in the third challenge. She killed the Minotaur and has just now made it safely through the labyrinth."

"Yes." Hades sat on his chaise lounge and regarded his fingernails. "I'm very pleased."

"She's proved she's capable of overpowering and killing a beast, but it's not her style. She doesn't want to kill the Hydra."

"Honorable trait."

"But you hated that very trait last summer."

"Death was deserved then; the Hydra is innocent and has loyally guarded the underwater entrance for centuries. I do not want her killed."

"Then why challenge Therese to do it?"

Hades gave Than a patronizing look.

"You expect her to fail. You want her to fail."

"I did. I don't anymore." He bit a cuticle and once again regarded his nails.

Than's mouth fell open. A ball of heat arose in his chest. It was hope. A flame of hope. He gripped his hands behind his back and waited for his father's next words.

"If she can make it past the Hydra into the Underworld through that entrance, she will have succeeded in the fourth challenge."

Than rushed to his father's side and took his hand. "Thank you."

Hades jerked his head back with surprise. Than released his father, awkwardly, realizing he hadn't touched him since he was a boy. He studied his father's face, waiting to be mocked, but instead was given the smallest hint of a smile on his father's lips, and for once the smile was not wry.

"I've just convinced Hermes to take your duties for two hours, so you can visit your red-haired girl in the flesh, as a reward for her accomplishment. You can clarify the fourth challenge to her then."

Than found Therese curled up in bed, her wavy red hair a dark gold crown across her pillow, shimmering and dancing as the sobs shook her and her dog, who sat up a moment later, wagging his tail. Therese looked at Clifford, perplexed, and then turned to Than with wide, red-rimmed eyes.

"Am I dreaming?" she asked in the scratchy voice of someone with a cold.

He shook his head, his feet heavy because he, too, could hardly believe they were together. They both gazed at each other for a moment, incredulous. Then she climbed from the covers, wearing her "Durango Demons" t-shirt and very short shorts, and folded herself into him, slinking against him like a cat, her hair slightly damp and smelling of oranges. She tucked her warm face against his neck, her breath tickling his skin. His arms closed around her as her body went limp.

She took in an audible breath. "It's really you."

He ran his hands along the small of her back beneath the thin shirt, having forgotten how soft she felt, how warm, how alive. She slipped her arms around his waist and looked up at him with the most beautiful round green eyes. Her lips parted into a sleepy smile.

"I can't believe it," she said. "How?"

"A gift from my father. To celebrate your victory."

A crease appeared between her brows as she sucked in her lips. Then she asked, "It was a victory, wasn't it?"

"What else would you call it?"

"Tragic." She buried her face in his chest.

He held her, stroking her soft, fine hair.

"I can't get rid of the image of them lying on the ground, dead because of me."

"I know. I'm sorry. They won't be dead forever. In a few days, they'll revive."

She looked up at him. "What about their bodies? What will the tourists think?"

"They're invisible. You could see them because they chose to show themselves to you."

She pressed her cheek against his heart. "Oh, Than. I don't know if I can ever kill again, even to save my life. It's such a horrible feeling. I've been absolutely miserable. But I've got to. I've got to in order to save you. It's crazy."

"You don't have to kill the Hydra."

She stopped sniffling and looked up at him again, her mouth agape. "What?"

"Hades likes that you don't want to kill for no good reason."

162

She gasped. "Really?"

The gleam in her eyes made his heart swell. "Really." Then he clenched his jaw. "But..."

"What?"

He held onto her, so she couldn't slip from him. He could already feel her lithe body sagging at the word "but." "You have to get past her."

"Her? The Hydra's a she?"

He nodded.

"What do you mean, "past her"?

He sighed and said, without inflection, "Why don't we sit down." He crossed to the chair beneath the window, pulling her into his lap. She curled against him like a newborn fawn—her knees against her chest, feet tucked beneath her bottom, arms around his neck. He wished he could hold her like this all night. Two hours wasn't enough.

"Well?"

He cupped her face in his hands and studied it, not having been this close to her—to the living, breathing, fleshy her—in so long. His fingers weaved into her soft hair of their own accord, and his lips sought hers.

Her next words to him were in prayer, because her lips were too busy kissing his, and he heard them as clearly as if she were speaking. "Oh, Than. I love you so much. I've missed you. I can't believe you're actually here, holding me, kissing me. God. Don't ever leave me again. I'll do anything. Anything."

He felt her tears touch his cheek, and he pulled back to wipe them from her face. "Don't cry."

"I'm so happy. And so sad."

"Me, too."

She stroked his face and gave him a sympathetic smile. Than couldn't recall a single time anyone had ever given him such a sweet look.

"I can't wait to be together like this all the time. Can you imagine? Can you imagine a time when my presence won't kill you, when you don't have to slay monsters and steal heavily protected golden apples just to be with me?"

Therese laughed that musical, lilting laugh that made his heart swell again. "I imagine it constantly."

He touched his forehead to hers, closed his eyes, and said, "We could do it now. Right now. Forget the last challenges."

"But the maenads."

All at once, Than was accosted by an onslaught of panicky prayer cries, "I couldn't be with you like that! I couldn't ask that of you! I'd rather break your heart than put you though a lifetime of such unbearable physical pain!"

He recoiled and searched her face. "What are you saying, Therese? Are you saying you'll refuse me if you fail the last challenges?"

She closed her mouth and pressed her face to his chest. Without speaking, she said, "I don't know. I just don't know."

Than's mouth went dry. He hadn't foreseen this. He'd been feeling afraid for her, afraid of the mortal pain and mental anxiety, but otherwise he'd been confident they'd eventually be together, one way or another. But now...was she really saying she'd refuse him?

"Let's please not think about that. Please let's just get me through these challenges."

"Look at me," he said, pulling her up by her arms, rising to his feet, frantic and angry. "Look at me!"

She lifted her eyes to his.

"You told me you would endure being burned to death to be with me. Isn't that right? Answer me."

She nodded.

"And were you telling the truth? Would you really do it? Suffer the most painful feeling imaginable just to be with me?"

She nodded again.

"And because I love you and respect you, I've agreed. I've agreed to allow you to make that sacrifice, because I believed you when you said you love me."

"I do love you."

"Then why won't you allow me to do the same: to make sacrifices to be with you? Man, Therese! I'm honoring your decision to accept the challenges. I'm honoring your decision to burn to death for me. Can't you honor my choice to face the maenads? Your love is worth so much more to me, and you're killing me!"

"I'm sorry." She shook her head, and he could see in her expression how conflicted she felt, how deep both her love and fear for him was, and he softened. "I'm sorry. It kills me, too. Thinking of that horrible pain every year forever. It kills me."

He pulled her to him and held her. She seemed too small and fragile to be fighting monsters.

"I won't fail," she said. "I will not fail. Tell me what I need to know to make it past the Hydra."

"Put on some warmer clothes and some shoes. And you'll want your traveling robe. I'll take you to her lair tonight so you can see what you're up against."

Chapter Twenty-Seven: The Hydra's Lair

Than held her hand, and together they god traveled, the invisible plastic wrapping itself around her, until she opened her eyes and found herself at the bottom of a massive grassy hill. Over a mile away, at the very top, was a structure she couldn't quite see.

"What's that?"

"It's a castle. Was a castle," Than said. "Nothing but ruins now."

"Where are we?" She used her hand as a visor against the just-rising sun—a strange sight when a few minutes ago, it was nearly midnight.

"Eastern side of the Peloponnesian Peninsula."

She punched his arm. "I suck at world geography. Can you be less specific?"

He laughed. "Greece. And this is Larissa Hill. Ancient Argos once stood here. The modern Argos is there, further down. See it?"

She turned around to discover hundreds of buildings and streets and cars, all modern and bustling with activity in the early dawn. "But where's the water? I thought the Hydra lived underwater."

"She does. Centuries ago, there was a lake here. Lerna. It's all dried up, but, if you look carefully along the base of this hill, you can still find signs of it."

"I don't understand."

"Beneath this hill lies a system of ducts. Most of the tunnels are dry or have a little water, maybe ankle deep. They connect several sinkholes."

"Sinkholes?"

"Little pools formed by underground springs that run from the Aegean Sea."

"Are you saying the Hydra lives beneath his hill?"

"Exactly."

"And the entrance to the Underworld?"

"Also beneath this hill."

She sucked in air and shuddered. "How do we get inside?"

He squeezed her hand and brought it to his lips.

"It's okay," she said. "I can do this. Tell me."

"You could crawl in through a tunnel, but since you have your traveling robe, we'll god travel in. Here's the thing, though: this hill is full of solid rock. You have to focus on a very specific location in order to be successful. That's why I want to take you with me first."

"So far so good."

"But..."

"There's a but?"

"Yeah. 'Fraid so."

She nodded, bracing herself.

"The Hydra could be anywhere. The tunnel I choose could be the very one she's hanging out in."

She lifted her eyebrows. "Great."

"So what I want to practice with you tonight, er," he looked at the sun-filled sky, "this morning, I mean, is split-second travel. I want you to learn how to leave a position before you've arrived."

"Huh?"

"You know that feeling you get when you god travel, that pressure all around you?"

"Like invisible plastic wrap."

"Okay. Plastic wrap? Or more like a thin blanket."

"A tight thin blanket," Therese added.

"Okay. Anyway, just as that blanket begins to release, before you've completely landed, inspect the location."

"You mean open my eyes?"

He took a step back and covered his heart with his free hand. "You've been traveling all this time with your eyes closed? Are you serious? You're lucky to be alive."

"But it's so bright."

"Not too bright. You can handle it. Promise me you'll keep them open from now on."

"I promise."

"Come on. Let's go over by those rocks. Ready?"

She nodded and squeezed his hand.

"Don't close your eyes, okay?"

"Okay."

"Focus."

"I am. Let's go."

The invisible plastic wrapped itself around her and she resisted the urge to close her eyes as brightness surrounded her from every direction. Before the plastic released itself, she saw the boulders coming into focus just as her feet were touching the ground.

"I could see!" she said when they landed. "I saw these rocks before we arrived!"

"Good. Now, what I want you to do is go back where we started, without me, but before you land, return here."

"How do I do that?"

"Just as the pressure gives, and you see that tall weed over there, will yourself back here by my side. You have to focus, okay?"

She nodded, releasing his hand. "Here I go." The pressure and brightness returned, but an image of Clifford on her bed entered her mind and she saw her room materializing around her. Before she landed, she thought of Than and the boulders, and she instantly returned to his side, but felt jolted, lost her balance, and fell on her bottom on the ground at his feet.

He cupped his hands beneath her armpits and helped her to her feet. "Not exactly what I had in mind, but looks like you're getting the idea."

"I went home, on accident." She dusted grass and dirt from the back of her traveling robe and jeans.

"I know. It's okay. If you need to get away from the Hydra, just go there, to your room. Any place is fine. You just want to get away, okay?"

"Okay."

"I want to take you into her lair and show you around. I want you to see the entrance to the Underworld, because if you can god travel straight there, then you might be able to slip inside without ever having to face the Hydra."

"That would be awesome."

"Yeah, but unfortunately, this little practice run of ours will make her angry and more alert. You'll want to wait a few days before you come back and try it on your own. Even if we get lucky and she doesn't spot us, she'll know we've been here by our scent."

"Great."

"Ready?"

"Don't let go." She took his hand, feeling less frightened than excited with him beside her.

The invisible plastic wrapped itself around her as the bright lights came from all directions. Forcing her eyes open, she saw the walls of the cavern come into view, but when they finally landed in a few inches of cold water, they were surrounded by complete darkness.

"I can't see," she whispered, clinging to his arm.

"Oh, I forgot. Humans can't see in the dark."

His body took on a soft glow, illuminating the tunnel a few yards in each direction. He looked amazing, like an angel. She whispered, "Wow."

"What?" he whispered back.

"Nothing." She felt herself blushing. "So, um, can you see in the dark?"

"Yeah. I guess you'll need to bring a light with you when you come on your own."

"Guess so."

"Now look here." He touched a thin column of rock beside him shaped like an hour glass and as tall as Therese. "Focus on this image when you travel here on your own, okay?"

"Got it." They were still whispering, hoping not to be heard by the Hydra.

"If the Hydra's waiting for you, go back to your bedroom before you land and try again another day, okay?"

"Okay."

"On the other side of this column is the sinkhole."

They sloshed through the shallow water to a heart-shaped pool about three yards in diameter.

"That's the entrance there."

"What, you dive in?"

"Yeah. You swim down a few feet and pop up on the other side, right into the Underworld. Ready?"

Something moved just beneath the surface as Therese peered at her and Than's reflections. Before she could speak, that something shot straight up—a long, serpentine neck ringed with scales that sparkled like abalone in Than's glow. At the top of the neck was an enormous dragon head with ferocious eyes and teeth, its mouth open and lunging for her.

She stared, frozen and heavy, unable to move. In the next instant, the pressure wrapped around her, and she and Than arrived back inside her bedroom, startling Clifford from his nap on her bed.

Than put his hands on her shoulders and studied her face. "You okay?"

She could tell her eyes were wide, her face pale. Nodding, she asked, "Was that…?"

"Yeah."

"I thought she had nine heads or something."

"Not anymore. Only one was immortal. Hercules slayed and seared the others."

"Oh." Not that it mattered. The one remaining head was big enough to eat her whole.

Than released her to pace the room. "If she's nesting in the sinkhole, you won't make it past her alive."

She couldn't imagine going back and looking over the heart-shaped pool, waiting, only to have that huge head pop out at her again. She'd nearly peed in her pants. "There's no way to tell where she is beforehand?"

"Not that I know of."

"What if I lure her away from the entrance?"

"How?"

"What does she eat?"

"Fish. But she loves cake, too."

"I could put a cake at one end of her lair. When I see her coming for it, I could god-travel to the heart-shaped pool."

He smiled at her as he took her in his arms. "That might just work, you clever girl."

"You'll need to take me in once more. To show me another place to god travel to."

"We'll practice as long as we can, but, first, kiss me."

Chapter Twenty-Eight: A Deadly Accident

Thursday morning after swim practice and lunch with Carol—Richard was out doing an interview—Therese hiked down to Jen's in the warm afternoon sun with Clifford trailing behind her. Stormy might not need to be groomed, but Therese needed to keep busy. Every idle moment added to her anxiety over what lay ahead.

It wasn't just getting past the Hydra, though that certainly would be enough to make anyone anxious. She did, after all, have to time getting in and out of the lair just right, which would be tricky, even after all the practice she and Than did last night. And apologizing to Vicki in the Underworld, well, that was less of a challenge than it was a gift, a gift of closure. Although the last two challenges worried Therese, what really had her stomach in knots was the part about burning to death.

Maybe her body would go into shock, so she wouldn't feel it. Maybe she'd burn quickly, and it would be over before she knew it. She shuddered and tried not to think about her flesh in flames.

Reaching the Holts' gravelly drive, now lined with cars belonging to trail riders, she headed to the barn as Clifford went on to the stream at the back of the house. Pete tapped his hat to her from the pen. She wiggled her fingers to him, and then to Bobby, who also waved. Jen was in the barn brushing Sassy.

Jen looked up as Therese entered. "Hey there."

"Hey. I let Clifford come today. Hope that's alright. He went straight to the stream, as usual."

"Sure. He never gives up, does he? Fishing for trout."

Therese chuckled. "Never." She took Stormy's brush from the shelf and sat on a stool in the front of his stall. He was getting big, though he still wasn't weaned, and he was sometimes skittish even around Therese. "It's okay boy." She stroked his soft gray hide and pressed her cheek against his flank. "Stormy. That's you, boy. You're Stormy. I'm Therese."

"Matt and I are going to the movies this weekend. Maybe you and Pete could join us."

"Hmm. I don't know."

"Think about it."

"Than and I are talking again. I was going to tell you the other day, but..."

"I thought you hated him."

"No. Not anymore. He's been busy trying to find a way for us to be together."

Jen came around from behind Sassy to work her other side. "So, do you really like him? I mean, 'like' like him?"

Therese nodded. "It's bad, Jen. I think I'm in love."

"No way. Y'all haven't even seen that much of each other."

"More than you know."

"What do you mean? He hasn't come up to see you, has he?"

Therese moved her stool so she could reach the backside of Stormy. "It was a quick trip. He flew in and out in one night. He's done that twice now."

"Is he loaded or something? That's a lot of money."

"I guess so." His father was the god of all precious stones, she supposed.

Just then, Bobby barged into the barn, breathless. "Therese, come quick. It's Clifford."

Therese and Jen exchanged worried glances as they left the stall and followed Bobby. Pete stepped from the pen holding Clifford's limp body in his arms.

"Clifford!" Therese ran to Pete's side.

"He slipped into the pen somehow. The General trampled him."

Clifford's head was a mangled mess, smashed and pouring blood. His little white and brown body twitched.

"He's not dead!" Therese insisted, a lump rising to her throat. "Can you take me to a vet?"

Pete met her eyes. "But..."

"Please?"

He nodded and carried Clifford to his truck. Therese and Jen followed to where it was parked in the garage, Therese no longer able to feel her arms and legs or the rise and fall of her chest.

Mrs. Holt came up alongside the truck as Therese blindly climbed in. "Listen, Honey. No use going to see a vet."

"You don' t understand. He's going to be okay." She said this with a quavering voice, sounding as unsure as she felt.

Bobby came up behind. "It's my fault. I'm sorry! When I opened the gate, Clifford ran past me! It's my fault!"

"No it's not, Bobby," Therese said.

Jen climbed in beside Therese, crying her eyes out. "I'm so sorry. I can't believe it."

"Get me a towel, Mom." Pete held Clifford at the opened passenger side door, blood running down his arms and onto his shirt and jeans.

"Thank you, Pete! Thank you for helping me!" In another life, she would have married him.

Mrs. Holt returned moments later with an old towel, which she wrapped around Clifford. It immediately became soaked with blood. "Ah, hell, let me get another."

"I'm so sorry," Jen said, more of a slobbering mess than Therese.

"It's okay. Clifford will be fine." At least she hoped. Artemis hadn't been angry enough with Therese to undo her gift of immortality, had she?

"Oh, Therese!" Jen cried. "Look at his head. He's not going to be fine!"

Pete lowered his eyes.

"Stop it!" she snapped. "I don't want to hear that." Please, Artemis.

Mrs. Holt returned with another towel, swaddling Clifford like a baby. Then she and Pete lay Clifford in Therese's arms. She cradled him, speaking softly to him, even though she could feel no life left in his body. He wasn't breathing, nor was his heart beating. He felt heavy with death, his stubby tail, usually wagging, stiff. "You'll be alright, soon, Clifford, boy. Hang in there."

Pete climbed behind the wheel and brought his truck to life. Tears streamed from Therese's eyes as she prayed over her best friend, silently. "Please let him be alright. Please, Artemis."

As they neared Therese's house, Carol ran from the gravelly drive, waving her hands for them to stop. Pete rolled down his window. Mrs. Holt must have called her.

"Is there room for me?"

Pete climbed out and helped Carol into the backseat of his truck. Carol leaned over and stroked Therese's hair. "Oh, sweetheart. I'm so, so, sorry."

"He's going to be okay. The vet will know what to do."

Therese sensed Carol and Jen exchange looks.

176

"Trust me, guys," Therese said as Pete drove across the dam. "Clifford will make it." She cradled his body like a baby as her teeth chattered. "Please hurry, Pete. He's losing so much blood."

She knew what they were all thinking. They were thinking, "Poor Therese. First her parents, then Dumbo, then Puffy, then Vicki, and now Clifford. Poor, poor Therese." But Therese knew Clifford could not die; at least, not forever. At some point, his soul would return to his body, just like Asterion and Ariadne's would. She wasn't sure how long it would take, but she hoped the vet could fix his head so his body would be ready when his soul returned. "Please, Artemis," she whispered, low, so no one could hear over the sound of the engine. "I beg you."

When they reached the emergency vet clinic, Pete dropped everyone off at the door, and Therese rushed Clifford inside. She was immediately led to an operating room, where a technician came in to exam Clifford.

"Let's lay him on the table," the young technician said as she pulled on gloves.

The stainless steel table was cold and hard. Therese kept her arms around Clifford as the technician carefully pulled the bloody towels away from Clifford's body.

"Oh, dear," she said, her eyes wide. She put one end of her stethoscope to her ears and the other to Clifford's blood-matted chest. "Tell me what happened."

"He was trampled by a horse," Therese said. "But he's going to be alright."

Carol shook her head. "Oh, Therese. She lost her parents only a year ago. This is hard for her to accept."

"Stop saying that, Carol!" Therese turned an angry face to her aunt, feeling the blood feverishly flow to her face. "This has nothing to do with my parents! This is totally different! You don't know everything!" Her heart raced fast. She couldn't breathe.

Carol backed away toward the door. The others lowered their eyes.

The technician wiped away some of the blood, gently handling Clifford's head. She pushed his lids down to cover his lifeless eyes. "I'll have Dr. Chenault take a look at him. Why don't you step out into the waiting room, and I'll call you back after she's had a chance to examine him."

"I don't want to leave him," Therese said. "The others can go, but I want to stay here."

Carol put a hand on her shoulder. "Therese, I..."

"Please," Therese said.

"That's fine," the technician said. "But I need the rest of you to clear the room. Thank you."

Carol kissed the top of Therese's head. "Sweetheart, I'm so sorry."

When Therese was left alone with Clifford, she wiped more of the blood away from Clifford's body. He'd stopped bleeding. His head was a clotted mess, and she could see the fractured skull and maybe even some of his brain behind his left ear. At least his eyes hadn't been crushed. She wiped each paw, rinsing one of the towels at the sink and wiping again— wetting, wiping, the whole time praying to Artemis, until, after about three or four minutes, Dr. Chenault entered the room.

The doctor, a thin, petite woman with curly brown hair and glasses, bent over the examining table and looked over Clifford, pressed her stethoscope to his chest, lifted the lids of his eyes and closed them again. "Poor guy didn't have a chance."

"I don't think he's dead. Can you try to revive him?"

178

The doctor narrowed her eyes at Therese and called her to the other side of the table. "Look here. See how his skull is collapsed? This kind of brain damage means he didn't suffer long. As soon as the hoof hit, this little guy was gone."

Therese wiped her eyes and nose with the back of her hand. "Can you fix him up? I don't care how much it costs. I've got a lot of money. Can you stitch up his head and make him look nice?"

"Do you mean like a taxidermist?"

Therese's mouth dropped open. "No. No, not like that at all." Her shoulders shook as a new wave of sobs constricted her throat and made it impossible to speak.

The doctor put a hand on Therese's arm. "I'm sorry."

One of Clifford's legs twitched. Therese covered her mouth with her hands and held her breath.

The vet saw it, too. "That's normal dear, especially with head injuries. That doesn't mean…"

Clifford blinked open his eyes and began to whine.

"What the…" The vet rushed to Clifford's side and looked at him closely. "He's breathing again. This is unusual. There's a pulse. His heart's beating."

Clifford started writhing and whining, obviously in great pain. Dr. Chenault had to hold him to keep him from falling off the table.

Therese gasped, not sure whether to laugh with glee or to scream in terror at his suffering.

"Call my tech back in here. Her name's Katie."

Therese ran to the door. "Katie! The doctor needs you!"

"You'll need to step out of the room, Therese. I'll update you when I'm done here. This is very unusual."

Therese met the others in the waiting room with a smile on her face. "He's moving around. I think he's coming to."

Jen jumped from her seat. "What?"

Pete crossed to her side and put a hand on her shoulder. "Are you serious?"

"What did the vet say?" Carol asked.

"It's very unusual."

Chapter Twenty-Nine: The Hydra

Dr. Chenault kept Clifford overnight on Thursday and Friday, but Saturday, after a disappointing swim meet, Therese rode with Carol and Richard to pick him up. He wore a hard cast on his head, covering all but his eyes and snout and would have to be fed a liquid diet with a turkey baster for a while. Therese suspected his skull would heal faster than most patients. After waiting a few more days for Clifford to get settled at home, she decided it was time to bake a cake for the Hydra.

She perused the pantry for a cake mix. Let's see, she thought. Chocolate, white, and yellow. Which would a monster like best? Chocolate was poisonous to dogs, but could it hurt a dragon-headed sea snake? She decided on her favorite—white cake with white icing—so if things went wrong, she could die eating it.

"What's the special occasion?" Carol asked when Therese slid the two round cake pans full of batter into the oven.

Therese had already prepared her answer: "I never properly thanked the Holts for Stormy." She realized then that she *should* bake a cake for the Holts, and she promised herself she would, if she succeeded in her fourth challenge.

Later that evening after dinner, she carried the cake up to her room, under the pretense of wanting to decorate it privately (which sounded weird and got her a funny look from her aunt), donned her sneakers, jeans, and traveling robe, along with her sword, shield, and visor with headlight, and god traveled to the foot of Larissa Hill near Argos, Greece. It was three in the morning there and dark, for the city was far below, like strands of white Christmas tree lights spread across an

181

enormous field, and though the stars and waning moon shone brightly, the hill was in shadows.

"I can do this," she said to the wind. She shivered in the cold. It was warmer when she came with Than at dawn several days ago. The night air chilled her to the bone. She should have worn a coat over the traveling robe. She could pop back and get one, but she decided to move on. "Let's get this over with," she said to no one in particular, or to any gods who might be watching.

She drew the sword, balancing the two-layers of cake in her left hand. Then, keeping her eyes open as she had practiced, she imagined the decoy zone located on the opposite side of the hill from the heart-shaped pool.

The invisible plastic wrapped around her, and the bright light shined from all directions. She recognized the fork in the tunnel with its peculiar anvil-shaped dividing wall. Since the Hydra was nowhere in sight, Therese landed at the fork, flipped on her headlight, set the cake on a rock near the ground, and then took several steps away from it to wait.

Her heart thudded in her ears as she ferociously bit the inside of her lips. The Hydra could come from any one of three directions—from either of the two tunnels that forked from the anvil-shaped wall, or from the main tunnel feeding into them, currently at her back. She sloshed around in the three-inches of ice-cold water, constantly turning to shine her light down each of the three ducts, both wanting and not wanting the monster to come.

She wondered if any of the gods were watching her crouched and shivering in the dark tunnel, her teeth now chattering uncontrollably as she held her breath, her limbs stiff, frozen with both cold and fear. She felt small beneath the massive hill and the ancient ruins, a tiny dot in the larger scheme of things. Realizing the gods would see her as nothing but a little frightened girl, she pulled her shoulders back, jutted out her chin, gritted her teeth, and narrowed her eyes. She was a warrior, and she would fight.

That is, if the Hydra would ever come.

As the minutes wore on, and the cold crept deeper into her bones, and the shivering made her feel like a victim of Parkinson's disease, she pondered the idea of calling out to the monster. She had tried and failed to study the petroglyphs carved into the rock throughout the tunnels. She had tried and failed to observe the tiny fish swimming near her feet. She had tried and failed to appreciate the stalactites, hanging like icicles from the ceiling. When she thought she could no longer take the cold, that she'd have to either pop back home for a coat or give up for another day, in a moment of insanity or delirium or both, she muttered, "Here Hydra, Hydra. Here Hydra, Hydra."

In less than a second, the water moved like the tide coming in across her calves, and a scream, like a train screeching to a halt, echoed throughout the tunnels. Therese couldn't tell from which direction the monster was coming. She spun around and around, dizzy and panting, telling herself to go, to leave, to get the hell out of there. But she couldn't focus. She couldn't imagine her destination, and this made god travel impossible.

Think, Therese! Focus!

In her spot of light, Therese saw the scaly beast, its huge dragon head bobbing up and down on the end of its long, serpentine neck. She also saw claws and legs and realized it wasn't a sea snake after all as it half slithered and half tromped through the water toward her. Eight other necks, four on each side of the base of the center one, hung seared and lifeless, flopping like wings. Therese stood with leaden feet, watching in terror wherever her light fell, her mouth agape and her mind blank and stunned. The great mouth opened, exposing rows and rows of sharply pointed teeth, and lunged toward her, its head now within inches of her.

183

Therese closed her eyes and thought of her room and Clifford nestled on her bed, but she didn't leave as the monster's snapping jaw grazed her nose before rearing back to strike again. Stupefied, Therese looked around in all directions, in full panic, swinging her sword madly, blindly, and hitting nothing. She leapt away from the path of the Hydra and fell on her hands and knees, her traveling robe ripped from her in shreds, hooked on the claws of the beast.

Therese sprang to her feet and retrieved her fallen sword as the monster discovered the cake and devoured it, making a noise sounding something like glee. Without stopping to look, Therese ran in the direction from which the Hydra had come, with only the circle of light to guide her. She stumbled once and fell, but scrambled to her feet, her eyes locked on the path before her. All she could do was run for her life. Even if she prayed, the gods couldn't help her.

At a fork in the tunnel, she went to the right, because the water seemed to get deeper the other way, and she knew the tunnel leading to the heart-shaped pool was shallow. The Hydra must have finished licking the icing from her mouth, for Therese heard the ground shaking again. She ran on, at full speed, but could hear the monster closing in on her, getting closer and closer to the shield on her back.

Another fork made her pause, and that was her undoing. If she'd flung herself one way or the other, she might have avoided being plucked up by the shield and lifted into the air. Therese threw her sword at the Hydra's head, slipped her arms from the shield, and jumped toward the rock wall. Scraping her hands and knees and elbows, she scuttled into a small cavity in the upper side of the wall, barely able to maneuver herself because it was a tight squeeze. She wriggled as far in as she could, flat on her stomach and elbows, until she hit up against solid rock. The Hydra screamed in frustration, chipping at the rock with her sharp teeth. Therese had nowhere to go and nothing to do but lie there.

"I will not freak out," she said aloud. "I will not freak out." She lay there, panting, trying to catch her breath, stuck like an insect in a spider's web, the walls closing in on her, like a cocoon, weaving tighter and tighter around her. The Hydra continued to scream and chip as Therese shouted, "Think!"

Using her hands and elbows, she rolled over onto her back to inspect her nook more fully, wincing with the realization that her back had been scratched by the claw of the Hydra. It stung and throbbed with pain now that she was aware of it. Up above her was another hole. She propped herself up, sticking her head into it, shaking so badly that her head repeatedly bumped into the rock. The light on her visor revealed another tunnel, so, like a termite, Therese pulled herself up till she was standing on her feet, cringing at the loud wails of the Hydra and the pounding against the rock near her. She unbelted her scabbard, useless now that her sword was lost, and let it drop to her feet. Then she grasped on to the rocks above her and found lodgments for her feet as she inched her way further up.

Therese rejoiced when she noticed the tunnel widening, allowing her to breathe and hold her arms out to each side. Eventually, she had to choose one side to scale, no longer able to stand astride the opening. She chose the side which was furthest from the wailing beast.

The wall became easier to scale, no longer upright, but slanting now into the steep slope of a hill, and the air became fresher, crisper. A few more strides, and Therese found herself safely out of the hill, staring up at the star-filled sky over Greece!

She emerged from the caverns and lifted her arms toward the moon, happy to be alive. She had been face to face with the monster and had lived!

Her elation quickly turned to dread as the pain throbbed in her back and she had this realization: if she left the hill now, she'd never have another chance to complete the fifth challenge. She had no traveling robe, and she had no way of getting another. She wasn't allowed to ask the gods for help, and they weren't allowed to help her, except to give advice. If she was going to make it through the entrance to the Underworld, she'd have to do it tonight. Besides, how would she get home without the robe? She might make it down to the city of Argos and ask for help, inventing some story about being abducted and taken to Greece. Then she wouldn't have to climb back into the cold and narrow lair and risk her life again. But that would mean no life with Than. He might insist on changing her anyway, but how could she live with herself knowing that her cowardice was the cause of his eternal torment?

She must succeed or die trying.

She took in another breath of the crisp, chilly air and then turned back to the hill, descending down the steep slope of the tunnel toward the Hydra.

As she bent her knees and hiked into the musty cavern, the quiet, still air made her shudder. The thrashing and wailing had stopped, and the beast could be anywhere. Therese turned her head in all directions, shining her light around the tunnel, not wanting to return the same direction she came. To her right, above a boulder wedged in the rocky slope, she spotted another opening. She inched over to it and discovered it was more gradual in its descent. Crouched low, she crept along as quietly as she could, following its curves as it spiraled down. When she reached a fork, she sat on her bottom and looked down both ways. If only one of the gods could give her a sign. This was worse than the labyrinth. She would never find the heart-shaped pool; she might as well find a needle in a haystack. Tears pricked her eyes, and she gave into the tears as they slid down her face.

Then she spotted water in the tunnel to her left, so she took it. Not long into the tunnel, Therese could stand, and a few yards further, the

186

walls opened up into a massive cavern, at least a hundred feet wide and twenty or more feet high. Shining her light all over the walls and ceiling, she lost her footing and fell into a body of water. She scrambled back to the bank, crawling on her hands and knees, and pointed her light on the water. It wasn't the heart-shaped pool. As she sat there catching her breath, she noticed something moving beneath the water, and the craziest idea struck her: the only way she'd ever find the heart-shaped pool was by having the beast lead her to it. If the Hydra nested there, she might return to it. So, without allowing herself to think twice, Therese climbed to her feet, and when the Hydra emerged from the water and slithered across the bank, Therese ran toward, rather than away, from her.

"Ahhhh!" Therese screamed as she ran, summoning the courage by burning her throat with the loudest sound she could muster. "Ahhhh!" she shouted again, and, surprisingly, the monster paused.

Therese leapt from the ground onto the scaly neck, and wrapped her arms and legs tightly around her. "Don't hurt me, don't hurt me, don't hurt me!" She closed her eyes, pressing her face against the slimy scales. The Hydra swung her neck back and forth, trying to buck her off, and, for a second, Therese compared the feeling to riding the octopus at the Pagosa Springs Fair.

Time for a new tactic, she thought in a lucid moment. "It's okay girl," Therese said softly. "There, there. I'm not here to hurt you."

The Hydra screamed back in reply and dipped down into the water. Therese held her breath and closed her eyes. When they resurfaced, Therese's light was gone and she found herself in complete darkness.

Down into the ice cold water they plunged, only to come up again. Down and up. Down and up. Therese shivered but clung to the neck, her ankles crossed, her right hand holding tightly to her left wrist. Apparently, the Hydra hoped to wash Therese from her neck by continuously dunking her underwater, but Therese fiercely held on. Then like the fastest rollercoaster ride ever, they streamed through the air, turning one way and then another, Therese gritting her teeth and clamping shut her eyes. Before she had a chance to take a breath, they plunged down into the water again.

The Hydra rolled round and round beneath the water, like an alligator, but Therese clung to the beast's neck with her arms and legs. Her neck and shoulders ached, and she trembled with cold, and now, she felt like she couldn't hold her breath much longer. She opened her eyes with panic and noticed a light glowing across from her. The memory of the night her parents died flashed through her. There had been a light then, too. But this light was different. It was a boy. A glowing boy. Was it Than? No, it was Hip, and he was swimming toward her!

She dived away from the Hydra and power kicked the dolphin kick to Hip. He wrapped his arms around her, and in the next instant, she was enveloped by sleep.

Chapter Thirty: Apollo

Than hovered helplessly above the Argos underwater entrance, ready to intervene and take Therese to his grandmother's winter cabin the moment she became mortally wounded. When her traveling robe got hooked on the claw of the Hydra, he cursed himself for not anticipating that possibility. Without god travel, she was doomed. But when she crawled from the hill, safe in the Grecian moonlight, he couldn't be happier, until he saw her turn back. She wanted to face the monster to spare him the maenads. His heart clenched with dread and love.

He couldn't believe his eyes when he saw her leap to the Hydra's neck and hold on. What was she thinking? Was she actually trying to befriend the beast? Was she cooing, "There, there"? This was crazy. He couldn't believe it. The Hydra could not be tamed. He wanted to reach down into the lair and shake Therese. Then he recoiled from the thought as he watched in horror: the Hydra thrashed Therese around like a loose, live wire.

He'd never seen the monster in such a panic. He couldn't recall anyone ever clinging to her neck like that. The beast flailed her head like a huge whip, but Therese held on, even underwater. The Hydra became more and more terrified the longer Therese held on, submerging herself again and again, hoping to free herself of Therese. Then she did the only other thing she could think of: she ran to her nest.

At last, Than realized Therese's plan, and, though he hadn't thought it possible, his esteem for her grew. He disintegrated and dispatched to the dream world to get his brother's help.

Than wished he could have been the one to meet Therese at the underwater entrance, but he couldn't risk weakening her further. Better for her to fall asleep anyway after sustaining so many injuries. When Hip took her in his arms and carried her to his field of poppies, Than saw the wound on her back and winced. He fragmented and dispatched to Mount Olympus to beg Apollo for help.

"He's not here," Artemis, Apollo's sister said, after Than addressed those present.

"Do you know where I can find him? It's an emergency."

"He's in Dallas with his boyfriend, who's running in a marathon today," Artemis replied.

Than thanked her and dispatched to Dallas, hovering above the city where the sun was now rising, until his eyes spotted a street filled with runners. Among them in mortal form was Apollo, running alongside another man. Than traveled to a copse of trees on the edge of the road, waiting. When the runners caught up, he fell in line beside the two runners, not in mortal form—he couldn't disintegrate and be in many places at once if he changed—but as a dimly lit god in a hooded track suit, hoping he wouldn't be noticed by the runners whose faces turned forward, focused on the road ahead.

"Can you be bothered, Cousin?" Than asked.

"For a price." Apollo's face gleamed with sweat in the light of dawn.

"Name it."

The next words by Apollo were prayed rather than spoken: "When this lover of mine perishes, hopefully many decades from now, give me time with him before you take him to the Underworld, and speak on his behalf to the three judges. He's a good man, deserving of the Elysian Fields."

"I swear," Than prayed back.

Apollo then turned to his lover. "Marvin, this is my cousin, Than."

190

The blond, trim man beside Apollo saluted Than, who dipped his head in reply.

"We've got a family emergency to attend to," Apollo continued. "Sorry to have to back out of the race. I'll see you at Monica's later."

"Sounds good," Marvin said.

Than and Apollo veered from the road and into more trees, Than saying, "My chambers," and together god-traveled to the Underworld.

On Than's bed, on her side, sound asleep, lay Therese, with Hip beside her. Than left as soon as he arrived to watch from a distance, so as not to endanger her life.

"The Hydra," Hip explained to Apollo.

The god of healing, and of music, and of many other things, hesitated. "My healing her won't implicate me in anyway, will it? Do we have your father's blessing?"

Hades appeared beside them. "Yes. She fought well and is deserving of your help."

Apollo laid his fingertips gently on Therese's wounds. The torn skin sought and found where it had once been joined and reunited into a seamless organ. He found other wounds on her legs and arms and healed them, too.

"She's a beautiful girl," he said when he had finished. "She'll make a lovely goddess."

Than felt his heart heat up like a spark ignited from stones. The hardest parts of the challenge were behind her, and now that she was healed, the excitement kicked in: soon, Dionysus would change her and they would spend eternity together. No more would he be forced to look at her from a distance. No more would he have to steal moments with her in her dreams. Never again would he have to beg and bargain to have his brother or Hermes take his place so he could be at her side. Soon, he would have unlimited access to her. They would spend all their days together. It occurred to him that though she must live with him in the Underworld, there was no reason why they couldn't travel the world together. Unlike his father, Than could disintegrate and be at many places at once, so while Persephone was forced to remain at Hades's side in the gloomy Underworld for six months out of the year, Therese could accompany Than anywhere. Why hadn't he thought of this before? Only now, had the possibility of her being his wife seemed real enough for him to fully contemplate. He'd never felt happier.

Of course, there was the problem of finding her a purpose. All gods and goddesses must perform a service, a duty to either humanity or to the world. If they were to be accepted on Mount Olympus, and if the transformation to immortality were to be permanent, Therese must find a purpose. He'd have to help her.

Before Apollo left, Than thanked the god of healing and music and assured him that he would keep his promise. Then he hovered above his chambers and took great pleasure in watching his future wife sleep.

Chapter Thirty-One: Preparations

Before Therese opened her eyes, she smelled him. Than's scent surrounded her as she stretched and yawned and hugged his pillow to her chest. In her mind, she prayed to him, "It won't be long now. One more challenge to go."

As she enjoyed the soft sound of the water cascading down the shelves of stone beside her, she wondered if she was supposed to begin the last of her challenges now. Could she find her way to Erebus on her own? There were two doors to Than's room: one led from his sitting room. The second must lead out to other parts of the Underworld. She walked across the room and to the second door, reaching out her hand. Strangely, her hand moved through the wooden door as though it were a curtain of light.

"This is odd," she muttered, but dismissed the anomaly as a typical occurrence in the Underworld and pressed the rest of her body through the door.

Light from the river of fire illuminated a narrow passageway, reminding her of the tunnels beneath Larissa Hill in Argos and the palace ruins in Crete. Just what she needed, she thought: another labyrinth. She followed the flaming river along the passageway, twisting and turning first to the right and then to the left and again to the right, the shadows on the walls and ceilings creeping her out and making her flinch more than once. Up ahead, she thought she saw someone turn a corner. She quickened her pace to catch up.

"Hello?" she called.

When no one replied, Therese moved onward, mentally sending out prayers to Than, Hip, and the Furies for help and guidance. "What am

I supposed to do?" she asked. "How can I succeed in the last challenge without directions?"

It was like trying to solve a puzzle with too many missing pieces, or to write with an inkless pen. This was crazy. This was ridiculous. But she pushed on through the tunnel, hoping for inspiration.

Therese turned another corner to find the path opened up to a large body of water, very much resembling the pool of water beneath Larissa Hill where she had leaped onto the Hydra's neck. A movement beneath the surface made her take several steps back. What appeared was not the Hydra, but Meg. Her blonde hair wasn't wet, as it should be, but long and curly, and blowing about her fiercely beautiful face, though no current moved through the cavern. A falcon rested on her shoulder, his feathers also dry. He stretched his wings with two quick motions, and then resumed his statue-like position at attention.

"Hello, Therese." Meg strolled across the surface of the water toward her. "I've been meaning to tell you how sorry I am that I was reluctant to accept you into our family. I'm afraid I wasn't very nice to you in Colorado. But I've been truly pleased with your performance and look forward to the day when I can call you my sister."

Therese clamped her mouth shut to keep it from hanging open and blinked several times to prevent her eyes from widening with surprise. Instead, she clasped her hands nervously behind her back. "Thanks, Meg. That's nice of you to say."

"As a token of my apology, I've brought you a gift."

"Have you come to tell me how to find Erebus?"

"No. Better." On either side of Meg, Therese's parents appeared, standing on top of the water, and smiling at Therese.

"Mom? Dad?" Therese stood in shock, her mouth agape without restraint. After a moment, she stumbled to the edge of the water, reaching out toward them, beyond excited by their presence. "It it really you?"

"Therese!" her mother cried out as she dashed to the bank and took her daughter in her arms.

Therese's father was close behind, enveloping the two of them in his warm embrace. "We've missed you so much."

Tears of joy sprang from Therese's eyes. "I didn't get to say goodbye. I've missed you like crazy. Does this mean I'm allowed to be with you again? When I complete the challenges, will we be together again?"

"I think so," her mother said. "But listen. There's something I need to tell you."

Therese looked at her mother with longing, breathing in her scent of Jergen's lotion and Haiku perfume. It lingered on her still. Therese was incredulous, absolutely in disbelief that her mother's arms held her again. And she felt warm, supple, alive—not cold, not lifeless. Her body felt like it always had when her mother had held her, rocked her as a child, sang to her on nights she couldn't sleep.

Her mother stroked Therese's hair. "We once told you we didn't want any more children, but that wasn't true."

"Really? I don't understand. If you wanted more kids, why didn't you..."

"We tried," her father said. "We tried and couldn't. So we were in the process of adopting. We were going to surprise you."

"Oh my gosh. I almost had a little brother or sister?"

"Almost, sweetie pie," her mother said. "And when we died, we wished more than ever that we hadn't left you alone."

"But I've had Carol."

"Of course. Thank goodness for her," her father said.

Her father's face looked exactly as it always had, his brown eyes warm, his smile gentle. She leaned in and smelled him, the musk of his cologne. The blankets on his bed and the clothes in her parents' closet had held that smell for months. Oh, how she missed it.

"I just wanted you to know." Her mother squeezed her tight. "I wanted you to know that we did try. Your father knew what it was like to be an only child, and it was important to him to give you pets and to keep trying."

"It's so nice to be with you again," her father said.

"You have your complete memory back, then?" First she took her father's face in her hands and examined it. "You remember everything about your past, the accident, me?"

"Why wouldn't I?" he said. "You're the best thing that ever happened to me."

Therese then took her mother's face between her hands and studied her mother's expression, felt her warm breath against her face. "Mom? You, too? You remember everything about our lives?"

"Oh, Therese! How could I forget? You're my most precious little girl!"

Therese wrapped an arm around each of her parent's waists and huddled there between them. "Once I marry Than, I'll spend every day with you. We'll be together again, like we used to be. Even Clifford can come. I can't wait! I can't wait to be with you like we used to be. Oh, Mom! Dad!" Tears fell rapidly down her cheeks and she thought she would burst with joy.

As she glanced back at Meg to thank her, something strange happened: Therese's hand fell from her arm and plopped onto the bank of the water. Then her ear slipped off the side of her face. "What's happening to me?" She screamed in terror. "I'm falling apart!"

Her parents picked up her hand and her ear and tried desperately to reattach them to her body, but they couldn't. Then the other ear slipped from her head, and she could no longer hear anything. "I'm falling to pieces," she said, just as a few teeth loosened in her mouth, and she had to spit to keep from choking on them. Holding tightly to her parents, she dreaded the new realization coming over her.

"No!" she screamed. "No! This isn't a dream! It can't be!" She wrenched her arms more tightly around her parents, even though a part of her knew they were silly, stupid figments.

She opened her eyes to find herself on Than's bed, and sitting on a golden chair looking at her was Hades, god of the Underworld.

"The human mind is an interesting thing," he said. "You not only reconstructed your original family, making it intact once again, but you also added an addition, so that the next time around—there really isn't a next time around, but humor me, will you?—so that the next time around you wouldn't be left alone. Your mind wants to correct what you perceive to be your parents' mistake: they should have given you a sibling, so when they died, you wouldn't be left alone."

"But I have Carol...and Richard. And there's Clifford and Jewels."

"Yes, yes, well. Good for you. But your mind longs for a more intimate connection to your parents, am I right?"

Therese sat up and stared blankly at the god, not sure if he was mocking her or sympathizing. "I suppose."

"You might find it interesting to know that they were not interested in having more children. In fact, though they loved and treasured you, they conceived you by mistake. Immediately after your birth, your mother had her tubes tied. She and your father never intended to have children because they worried their careers would take too much time away from parental responsibilities."

Therese felt her face go pale, her stomach queasy.

"They loved you dearly, of course, and never regretted having you. I'm giving you this information because I want you to understand why they didn't have more children."

"Because they never intended to have any."

"But they loved you. Remember that."

She nodded, wishing he hadn't told her she'd been a mistake.

"Listen to me, Therese, because I've said this many, many times to many, many mortals, and it always seems to go in one ear and out the other—hence your ears being among the first parts of your body to fall off in your dream. Interesting symbolism. Wouldn't you agree?"

She frowned.

"I've lost count of how many times I've said this. Even the gods don't know how many. Once a mortal dies, he or she cannot come back, though there have been rare exceptions. This means that, should you succeed in the fifth challenge—and we're all rooting for you now, dear girl, really, we are. You're performance has been impressive. A pleasant surprise. So, should you succeed in the fifth challenge, you will not be reunited with your parents as you dreamed. They are happy in the Fields of Elysium, but believe me when I tell you they do not remember you. Their memories have left them and cannot be restored. Look at me, Therese."

Therese, who had looked away to fight tears, forced herself to meet his eyes. She was surprised to see kindness, compassion, and acceptance. As he tugged his curly, black beard, his dark eyes bore into hers like those of her swim team coach, of her spelling bee sponsor, of her own mother and father—of every adult who had ever advised or counseled her. He wanted her to succeed.

"I want to warn you about a few characters whose paths you may cross on your journey to Erebus. Each of the five rivers is inhabited by at least one nymph, and they are mischievous creatures who will try to

198

distract you. Pay them no mind, but be polite. If offended, they can impede you."

"Okay. Thanks."

"In addition to the nymphs, there are other daemons that dwell here. You've met my daughters, the Furies. The Fates are also here, though they will not likely try to speak with you. Usually mortals wish to seek them out to bribe them into changing their destinies."

"Can they do that?"

"Not without a price that's usually too difficult to pay."

Therese swallowed hard.

"I also have a vulture, Euronymus, who flies though the tunnels coming and going. He strips the flesh from the uneaten human corpses. He won't bother you, but he may screech by and bulldoze you down—he's as big as you are—so be on the lookout. Ascalaphus, my owl, may also screech or hoot as he flies about the caverns. He's friendly. No worries there. And, of course, there are other creatures that lurk here—bats, spiders, snakes, and such."

"I'm not afraid of them." She was elated by how obvious it was that he really did hope she would succeed, but she didn't dare smile. He frightened her still.

"One more thing, Therese. Every mortal whom I have ever allowed to descend down here to speak with the dead has been told to return to the land of the living without looking back. I ask this of them as a sign of trust. Orpheus, above them all, seemed the most likely to succeed. Of them all, I thought he had a chance. But at the last minute, he, like everyone before and after him, suspected me of cheating him, of tricking him in some way. He looked back to make sure I was keeping my end of the bargain. Believe me when I tell you I was disappointed. Crushed, really. I loved Orpheus. His music filled me with happiness. I tell you this because you and Than seem confident that the challenges are

199

essentially over. All you have to do is journey down to Erebus and apologize to Vicki Stern. Then you must turn back to the gates, board Charon's raft, and allow him to return you to the Upperworld. That all sounds easy, but here's the rub: You shall not look back. Do you hear me? Ares will try to trick you, do you understand? I can do nothing to prevent his interference. You must not look back. In case I'm not being clear, let me say once more: YOU MUST NOT LOOK BACK. Do you understand?"

Therese nodded dumbly.

Hades rolled his eyes. "I doubt this little talk of ours has done any good. I can only hope. If I could take back the challenge I would, dear girl. But you must complete it. Are you ready?"

"Now? Right now?"

"There's no better time than the present, as they say."

"Yes. Yes, I'm ready."

"Follow the Phlegethon—that's the river of flames—until it crosses the Lethe. At that junction, turn right and follow the Lethe down to the edge of a deep cavern. If Charon comes by on his raft, you may ask him to take you into Erebus; otherwise, you will have to scale down the walls yourself. But you can do it. I've seen you climb. Once you apologize to Vicki, you can either catch the raft back, or, if you don't want to wait for Charon, you'll have to climb back up. Don't come back this way, though. Follow the Lethe in the opposite direction, toward the Styx. Turn right at the Styx. It will take you to the main gate, where Cerberus sits on guard. Wait on the bank for Charon. He'll take you on the raft by way of the Acheron. Although you'll come out at what will look like the middle of a desert, don't worry. If you succeed, I will fetch you myself and take you to Dionysus."

"And if I fail?"

"If you fail because of mortal injury, you will stay here. The judges will determine precisely where. If you look back—and, please, Therese, don't look back—then Hip will carry you home to Colorado, as you sleep."

"I won't look back."

Chapter Thirty-Two: The Final Challenge

As Therese stepped through the wooden door of Than's room—opening it, for it was solid, unlike it had been in her dream—she wished again Hades hadn't told her the truth about her parents. She hated the idea that she'd been an inconvenience to them, a burden, even if, later, they loved her. Therese emerged into a tunnel similar to the one in her dream, and for a moment she worried, actually wished, it was another dream. If she were dreaming, then what Hades had said about her being an accident might not be true. She pushed off the ground with her feet, but landed squarely on her sneakers. Pinching herself brought no change. As far as she could tell, she wasn't dreaming.

The tunnel opened onto a larger cavern, and as soon as Therese stepped inside, a coven of bats was disturbed and rushed in a whirlwind around her before making its escape through a tight opening above. The coven consisted of thousands, perhaps even hundreds of thousands, of small fruit bats similar to some she had seen once with her parents and grandparents at an abandoned train tunnel near San Antonio.

Hades had warned her there were creatures, but hundreds of thousands? Maybe Ares had multiplied them in an attempt to scare her. You'll have to do better than that, Ares, she thought.

Had that been a thought or a prayer? What was the difference between the two, especially when one addressed a god? Hoping Ares had no privy to the thought, Therese hiked on along the river of fire. The last thing she needed was for the god of war to feel challenged.

As she hiked, she thought again of her parents and their plan not to have children. Had the accident not occurred she wouldn't exist. At all?

Not even here, or in heaven, or somewhere else? How strange her existence, her whole being, depended on one unplanned act.

People say things happen for a reason and things are meant to be, so maybe she came along in spite of her parents' wishes. She was destined to live, to meet Than, and to be here, right now, at this moment. Or, maybe life consisted mostly of accidents and there was no plan, no destiny. Maybe you had to make your own destiny.

Hades said her parents had no regret about having her. How could he be sure? What if there were moments when her parents wished they didn't have to compromise their careers in order to take care of her?

She wondered if it would be possible to see them, even though they wouldn't recognize her. The dream had seemed so real and had felt so awesome. Maybe she would pass by the Elysian Fields and catch a glimpse of them on her way to Erebus. Maybe.

The passageway turned sharply to the right, and as she followed it, a swarm of rats ran down the ceiling and onto her. They weren't biting, so she didn't panic. She had often wanted rats for pets because she had learned, after her parents got her Puffy, that hamsters were generally antisocial, whereas rats loved human company. She had played with rats at the pet store in town and had tried to convince Jen to get some—you should never get just one, because they get lonely and need companionship, the pet store worker had said. Now, as the rats crawled up her arms and legs, along her shoulders and the front and back of her neck, she giggled.

"That tickles." She lifted one with both hands—you should never lift a rat by the tail, she recalled, because you could injure its spine—and looked into its beady eyes. They were red because of the reflection of the river of fire. She imagined they were black otherwise. "Hello there," she said to it.

One rat made its way beneath the leg of her jeans, so she bent over and grabbed it with her other hand. "Oh no you don't, mister." Meanwhile, several were burrowing in her hair and licking her earlobe. "I have to get going guys. Are you coming with me?" She set the two in her hands down on her shoulders.

Carefully, so as not to step on any of them, she moved forward. Most ran from her limbs and hair, but a few lingered on her shoulders and the back of her neck, their tails clinging to her face for balance. She spit when one of the tails moved across her lips. Otherwise, their company wasn't so bad.

Jen would freak, she thought.

All but the two perched on her shoulders eventually scurried away. She was glad for their company, especially as she neared the junction where the river of fire met the Lethe, and before she could turn right, away from the flames, a beautiful woman with long green hair and flowing robes of the same hue emerged to the surface of the river and smiled at her.

Therese smiled back, unsure whether she should stop or keep going. Recalling Hades's warning to be polite, she stopped and said, "Hello."

"Hello. Who are you?"

"Therese. And you?"

"Lethe."

"I thought Lethe was a river."

"Indeed. It's named for me. Why are you passing this way?"

Therese wasn't sure whether she should tell the whole story, but when she considered that it might win the woman's sympathy, she decided to tell all. "Thanatos and I are in love and want to marry, but in order to be accepted by Hades, I have to complete one last challenge of five."

"Oh? Why would such a young lady wish to join the daemons of the Underworld?"

Therese looked about her. "It's actually pretty fascinating down here. And, as I said, I love Than."

Lethe asked her more about her life, about the challenges, about how she came to know Thanatos. When she seemed satisfied with Therese's answers, she asked one more.

"Do you miss your parents?"

"Of course."

The woman floated on the river with only her head above the water, and her long green hair streamed behind her like fishing line carried by the current. "It hurts, doesn't it," she said without inflection.

"Yes. Very much."

"I can help you with that pain."

"How?"

"I can help you forget. Think how much happier you'd be as Than's wife if you didn't have to be burdened by that feeling of loss for all eternity. Wouldn't you rather be happy?" Lethe floated right up to Therese, her face only a foot away, and smiled. "We'd all like to be happy. Happy forever, Therese. Wouldn't you like that?"

It sounded lovely to Therese just then, and she felt her body relaxing. She could forget how badly she had let Vicki down, how she should have died, too. She could forget about her parents' death, about all her losses. Lethe began humming a soft melody, soothing Therese, making her shoulders relax for the first time in months. The rats on her shoulders sat very still as the peace beckoned her.

"Don't you want to be happy? Forever?" Lethe asked again, smoothly. "All you have to do is take a sip of the river; or, better still, take a swim with me and feel its refreshing current move through you, giving you a new life."

"A new life?"

"That's right, Therese. Doesn't that sound nice?"

Therese nodded. The shame over Vicki and the longing for her parents could be erased with one small sip, or one restful dip. Then she could marry Than and live happily ever after.

But would she remember Than? Or would a sip from the Lethe wash away all her memories?

And did she really want to forget her parents altogether, as though they had never existed?

The thought of losing all recollection of her parents made her throat tighten and her shoulders tense. The two rats fled down her arms and legs and disappeared.

"Thanks, Lethe, but I don't want to forget."

The goddess rose from the river, a giant, as tall as Todd's truck, and looked down at her. "Come with me, Therese. Only I will make you happy!"

Therese turned from the goddess and ran, following the river, which flushed white in ripples, like bursting pipes, as she passed it. As she ran away from the river of flames, the cavern became darker, and if she hadn't slowed because of the darkness, she would have plunged into the canyon below. As it was, she teetered on the edge, struggling to regain her balance. She plopped on her bottom, panting and gritting her teeth, hoping this was all nearly over. Please, she prayed. Please let this be over soon. She stared down the canyon wall and sighed with relief when she recognized Erebus in its purple glow.

Although the canyon was deep and narrow, it spread out near the bottom where hundreds of souls lay around with half-closed eyes in a shallow pool of the Lethe, which trickled down the canyon wall like water from a faucet that hasn't been properly closed. Hades had said she could scale down to the bottom to look for Vicki, but she was worried about falling into the water and erasing her memory. She sat with her legs dangling over the edge, watching for Charon and his raft.

In the next instant, she felt something tickle the back of her neck. Thinking it was one of the rats, she reached back to pick it up when her hand wrapped around the slimy body of a snake. She threw the snake across the cavern, unsure whether it was poisonous, and climbed to her feet. The snake, which had landed only a few yards away and which looked to be about four feet long, curled into a tight coil and lifted its round head to look at her. She studied its black opened mouth and grey scales, trying to identify it, slowly backing away from its head, now recoiled as though about to strike.

Within seconds, the grey monster leapt into the air toward her face. Therese jumped back, the snake barely missing her as it fell to the ground. As the snake coiled and lifted its head for another go, Therese careened through the air, her knees suddenly wobbly. She looked all about and discovered she was standing beside Charon on his raft sailing through the air toward Erebus in a downward spiral.

She couldn't be happier to see the old god, his bright bald head and slender, bowed frame. He held his long pole in both hands, circling it to their left, the center of their spiral. Soon they hovered above the shallow pool, unnoticed by those lying in it. Charon pointed one long bony finger across the canyon. Therese turned in the direction he pointed to see Vicki on the edge of the pool only a few yards away.

Vicki sat on the edge of the pool surrounded by others, but Mrs. Stern wasn't one of them. Her face was mostly expressionless except for a hint of sadness in her eyes, which stared off in a daze. Tears streamed down Therese's own eyes as she again wished it had been her instead of her friend who'd died. She couldn't stand the thought of Mr. Stern being all alone, heart-broken, for the rest of his life.

207

Therese looked once more at Charon, whose face remained impassive. Afraid to step from the raft, she cupped her hands around her mouth and shouted, "Vicki! Vicki Stern!"

Nothing happened. No one even looked in her direction.

Did Vicki even remember her own name? How could Therese apologize for something her friend no longer remembered? Maybe this apology wasn't about Vicki. Maybe it was the only way Therese could come to terms with what happened—to accept responsibility for her part. Maybe she'd feel better after. Maybe she'd prove to Hades she'd learned a lesson.

While she was pondering these thoughts, the three Furies appeared floating above the pool of water between Therese and Vicki. "Apologize!" they shouted, blood pouring from their eyes. Their hair lifted up into coils of slithering snakes as they grew closer to her. "Apologize!"

"Um…"

Blood dripped from their lips. Alecto's hands reached for Therese's neck, wrapping cold fingers around her throat. "Apologize!"

"I'm sorry!" Therese cried, her voice only a squeak beneath the pressure of Alecto's fingers. "I shouldn't have bought the drug! I hate that I'm still alive and you're not! I hate what I did and wish I could take it all back! Oh, Vicki! Look at me!"

To her surprise, Vicki sat up and turned to look at her.

"I'm so sorry!"

Vicki first bent her brows; then she smiled and waved. "It's nice to see a friendly face."

"Do you remember me?"

"Should I?"

"Are you okay?"

Vicki shrugged. "I felt sad for a long time, but I'm feeling much better. They say around here that I'm due to leave this place soon. Supposedly there's a much prettier place. Are you going there?"

"One day, maybe."

The Furies disappeared and the raft spiraled upward. Therese fell to her knees, aghast by what had just happened, bewildered by the Furies' treatment of her, relieved by Vicki's smile, and dizzy from the circling movement of the raft. She silently thanked Hades as they sailed above Erebus and then swiftly turned down the Lethe in the opposite direction from where she came. Water jumped up at her from the river, threatening to touch her, and in so doing, wipe away some of her past. They sailed so quickly, the underground scenery was a whirlwind. Therese prayed to Hades, to Than, to Hip, and to all the gods to help her even though she knew they weren't allowed to come to her aid. The raft swiftly turned again, and now they flew along the blackest of the rivers—the Styx. Therese thought she saw a pair of eyes in the water looking up at her alongside the raft, following them, but before she could bend closer to the water, they stopped at the black iron gate, just on the inside, where Charon pointed to the bank and waited.

"I'm to get off here?"

He continued to point, though his face remained without expression or reply.

Therese climbed from the raft and waited near the gate, careful not to look back, but relieved she had made it to the end. She could see Cerberus just on the other side as Charon passed him.

"Therese!" someone called from behind her. It sounded like the voice of her father. "Therese, don't look back. Just listen to me! Hades has sent us as a gift."

"Sweetheart!" This was the voice of her mother. "We've been allowed to hug and kiss you, but that's all. Be careful not to look at us."

"What? Is that really you, guys? You can remember me?"

A hand touched her shoulder.

"We couldn't for the longest time, but Hades has given you this gift. You're allowed one moment to be with us again."

She felt arms wrap around her waist from behind, and a kiss was planted on the top of her head. "We love you so much," the voice of her father said. "It's so good to be close to you again."

"I miss you, sweetheart."

Therese's teeth began to chatter and her knees felt weak. "That can't be you, can it?" She wanted to turn to look at them so badly. What if Hades really did wish to reward her with this gift? "I miss you, too," she said feebly.

"We can't wait to see you again," her father's voice came behind her. "You've grown so much, in just a year. How are those chipmunks doing? Are you remembering to feed them the seeds I bought?"

She wanted to turn to see her father's face, to touch her mother's cheek!

"No!" she shouted without turning, shutting her eyes closed. "Whoever you are, you aren't my parents! I'm not falling for it!"

"You can take us with you," her father said more gently. "Hades even admitted that there have been rare exceptions to the rule that mortals can't return from the Underworld. Why can't we be one of those exceptions? Thanatos loves you, for heaven's sake! Who better to be granted an exception?"

Therese paused. That was true. If any exception could be made to the rule that mortals could not return, why couldn't one be made for her parents? If Than loved her, what stopped him from demanding this favor of Hades?

But this had to be a trap. Ares was trying to get her to look back. She wouldn't fall for it. "Leave me alone! If you are my parents, leave me alone, and, if it's possible, I'll come back for you once I'm a god."

"We understand," her mother's voice cried. "Don't look at me, but come and give me one last kiss."

Therese fixed her eyes on the gate and shouted, "Figments, I command you to show yourselves!"

A fluttering of wings sounded behind her, but she dared not turn to see what it was. After a moment, she heard only the sound of the river lapping against the bank.

Up ahead, Charon circled across the Acheron where she could see Than boarding with two others. They sailed back to the Styx and past Cerberus. The great gate groaned open as the raft came toward her. She waved to Than and called out his name. The look he gave her puzzled her. Here she was at the end of her final challenge, and his expression was more apprehensive than ever. What was wrong?

She watched him sail past her, and then, without thinking, she turned and followed him with her eyes as he sailed into the Underworld.

Her hand flew to her mouth, and she immediately turned back toward the gate, hoping no one had seen, but knowing they must have. Of course they'd seen! She dropped to her knees, begging any god who'd listen to have mercy on her.

Then Than appeared. "Do you want to do this thing?"

"You mean burn to death?"

"Yes."

"But the maenads." She felt herself losing consciousness.

"Forget the maenads. Will you burn?"

"Yes."

Chapter Thirty-Three: Demeter's Winter Cabin

Than fragmented and flew to Therese, and, with her consent, scooped her in his arms, and traveled to his grandmother's winter cottage in a heavily wooded area near the base of Mount Kronos. As soon as he arrived, he laid Therese on a bed and left the house so as not to further endanger Therese's life. Once he was a safe distance away, he hovered above the cabin ready to explode with frustration. Therese had almost succeeded. If only she hadn't spotted him, she would have left through the gate and become his queen, accepted by the other gods, rather than exiled from Mount Olympus for all eternity. He'd tried to issue her a look of warning, to remind her of Hades's one command—do not look back—but his expression had only bewildered her into watching him. He bellowed out his frustration, shaking the woods below. Birds darted from their nests, rabbits dashed into holes, and even humans turned their heads up to the sky, looking for thunderclouds. The tears gathering in his eyes fell like rain on a few treetops. He bit his tongue so hard it bled. So close. She had been so close.

Demeter and Persephone arrived moments later, also full of tears, but not for Therese. They flew to where he hovered above the cabin and threw their arms around him.

"They'll rip you to pieces," his mother said through thick sobs.

"And not just once," his grandmother added. "But every year."

His mother cupped his face in her hands. "Please don't do this, Thanatos. I beg you, as the mother who gave life to you. I beg you with all my heart. Your pain will be unbearable, but so will mine when I hear your cries each year forever."

"Please, Thanatos," his grandmother added. "Heed your mother's words. Those who love you will suffer for all eternity. Love is fleeting. Punishment for broken oaths is not."

Thanatos pulled back from their suffocating embraces. He loved them, but this was hard enough without them reminding him every minute of every day. Having his one thumb ripped from his body had hurt like hell. Multiply that by a thousand. He shuddered. Yes, he knew what they were saying made sense, but he had to have Therese. "You don't understand. Without her, I have no life. If you don't want to suffer over my pain, then stop trying to talk me out of this thing. If I don't do it, I'll be miserable. With Therese at my side, you may hear my cries once a year; without her, they'll be constant. If you love me, give it to me now."

Demeter pulled a vial from the folds of her robe and reluctantly handed it over to Than. "The more you rub over her, the faster she'll burn. Use it all to ensure a speedy death."

"And son, you can't take her soul from her body. If you do, the process is ruined."

Than's mouth dropped open. "But all along I planned to take her before I set fire to her body."

Demeter lowered her eyes. "I'm sorry. It won't work if you do."

"Maybe now you'll change your mind?"

Than chewed his bottom lip, which, like his tongue, trickled with blood from his own doing. "Therese must decide. Please go and put the question to her."

Chapter Thirty-Four: Burned Alive

Therese awoke in a strange room, feeling dazed. Her throat was tight and dry, and she was overcome with a desperate thirst.

"Water," she muttered to anyone who might hear. "I need water."

Demeter appeared beside her, her long corn-blonde hair in two braids wrapped in buns on each side of her head, a little too high to resemble those of Princess Lea from *Star Wars*. The goddess handed Therese a golden goblet. Therese sat up and drank greedily.

Once satisfied, she looked around the room. The cabin was rustic and quaint, with windows on three sides and a kitchen and table across from her where she sat on the only bed in the room. Two closed doors might have led to other rooms.

Therese took another swallow of the fresh, cold water, and then gave the goblet back to Demeter. "Thank you."

"You're welcome." Demeter laid the cup on the table and turned back to Therese. "It seems you have a very important decision to make, young lady."

"I do?"

Demeter took a seat in a chair at the table across from the bed and narrowed her eyes at Therese. "Yes. The lives of many others will be affected by your choice, so choose wisely."

"Yes, ma'am."

"As you know, you failed the last challenge set to you by Hades."

Therese lowered her eyes. She'd been so stupid. After fighting the urge to look at her precious parents, she lost her mind and forgot what she was doing for a split second as she watched Than enter the Underworld.

214

"I can't believe it." Tears welled in her eyes and she sniffled. "I'm so sorry. I was so stupid."

"You were set up to fail."

Therese lifted her head and searched Demeter's face. "What? How?"

"When Ares's plan of luring you with the voices of your parents failed, he sent his sons, Fear and Panic, to arouse your worry over Than."

Therese jumped to her feet. "But that's not fair!"

"Life rarely is."

Therese stared back, her mouth agape, letting it all sink in. Deflated, she muttered, "But death is," and sank back down on the bed.

"You know what will happen if Thanatos follows through with his plan to give you immortality."

Therese had tried so hard. She'd given each challenge her all. She risked her life to spare Than. The tears of frustration overwhelmed her as she covered her face with her hands. "I did everything I could! I tried so hard! I got past the Hydra, for crying out loud! Can't I have another chance? Can't I do something else to show I'm worthy?"

"Hades knows you're worthy, but, as he would say, 'A deal is a deal.' The laws of the challenge are immutable, and now, you must deal with the consequences."

"Why is it that so many exceptions have been made throughout history and none can be made for me?"

"Even those exceptions required a terrible price. Nothing in life is free."

Therese absently rubbed her tired legs as she muttered, "I can't let Than suffer for all time."

Persephone appeared beside them. "Thank you, dear girl. I'll take you home when you're ready."

215

"Wait," Demeter ordered. Looking at Therese, she said, "If you don't accept Than's gift of immortality, he may suffer just as horribly as he would if you do. Perhaps more."

"But," Persephone objected, "he may not. Maybe he will for a year or two, and what are they to a god? There's a good chance he'll get over Therese and move on with his life and never suffer again."

Than's voice boomed throughout the house: "Can you hear me Therese?"

She climbed to her feet and turned her face toward the ceiling. "Than? Where are you?"

"I'm close. Listen to me."

She nodded, shifting her weight nervously from one foot to the other, again and again.

"I love you more than I know how to say, and, more than anything, I want you at my side. But..."

She laughed nervously. "There's a but?"

"Originally, when I agreed to make you into a god, I thought, since I'm Death, I could take your soul just before I set you aflame, sparing you the pain of burning alive. But my mother and grandmother have just informed me doing so will ruin the transformation. This means that, if I were to go through with this, you would have to endure unimaginable pain. So, my question is, do you still choose to join me under those conditions."

Therese pulled at her hands, looked briefly at each of the goddesses in the room with her, and then turned her face back up to the ceiling. "Than, I already expected to feel the pain, so that changes nothing for me; what does affect my decision is the cost of my failure to you."

"Do you promise that is your only hesitation?"

"Yes. Absolutely. Definitely."

"Leave us!" Than's voice boomed. In the next instant, the two goddesses vanished, and she was alone in the cabin with him. He looked into her eyes, cupped her head with his hands, and pressed his lips to hers.

Her knees gave out, and he lifted her in his arms and laid her on the bed.

"I'll try to make this quick," he whispered at her ear, his breath warm and sweet.

He tugged off each of her sneakers, letting them drop to the floor. He unrolled her socks, quickly, and tossed them down with her shoes. Then he unbuttoned and unzipped her jeans.

"What are you doing?" she asked weakly, trembling with fear, her entire body erect with goose bumps.

"I have to undress you, in order to anoint you with the ambrosia."

"Oh."

He leaned over her and pressed his mouth against her cheek, feverishly working his mouth down her throat as he unbuttoned her shirt. She helped him by pulling her arms from the sleeves, unable to hide her trembling as he tossed her shirt in a heap on the floor with her other things. She lay on the bed in nothing but her bra and underwear.

"You're so beautiful," he whispered. "I'm so sorry for what I'm about to do."

She felt weak—whether from his presence, so lethal to her, or because of the tremendous fear she felt, she didn't know. She managed to mutter, "It's nothing compared to what you'll have to go through. Oh, please. Let's just get this over with. I'm thinking of us together. Forever." Her teeth began to chatter on that last word, and her body jerked and twitched, as though it were freezing.

He took a vial from his pocket and opened it. He poured the smooth liquid onto his hands. It reminded Therese of Jergen's lotion, and she thought of her mother, and then of her aunt Carol. She wondered if she'd ever see her aunt again, and this thought made her cry again.

Than rubbed the ambrosia first on her legs and feet. Therese tried vainly to pretend she was having a body massage, like she and her mother had done a few times in town, but nothing she thought of could help her body to relax and stop its fretful twitching and jerking and chattering.

Next, he rubbed the ambrosia on her arms and hands. As he did so, he said again and again how much he loved her and how grateful he was to know her. In spite of her fear and weakness, and now a shortness of breath and tightening of throat, Therese actually felt the pleasant pulse of desire and arousal when his hands moved to her shoulders and collarbone. He swept his hands quickly along her stomach, then her face. Then beneath her, along her back, his hands swept in long, gentle strokes. She found herself distracted by a desire for him to touch her in other places, too. She closed her eyes and actually sighed with pleasure when he finally did. She knew he couldn't linger anywhere because her life was already extinguishing due to his presence, but his soft touch, however rushed, gave her a taste of something to look forward to and something to think about other than burning alive.

When he'd finished, he carried her nearly naked body from the cabin and onto an altar beneath the bright blue sky. Though she was weak and short of breath and trembling with fear, she noticed the birds flying overhead and the sun setting behind the mountain. The wind blew, not too hard, but not gently, and Therese had this sickening thought: the wind would help her burn quickly.

She gritted her teeth and prayed, "Oh, god, oh god," repeatedly to anyone and everyone who might be listening.

Then Than lit a match.

"I love you, Therese," he cried as he put the flame to her hair. "May you go quickly."

Then, as she watched her hair light up in thick, hot flames around her face, she was surprised to see Than pour kerosene over his head and entire body and then lay beside her on the altar and throw his arms around her.

He was going to burn with her!

"I love you!" he cried again.

The flames reached her scalp, and sharp, intense pain spread across her skin. In the next instant, Than's entire body was a flurry of flames. She resisted the urge to struggle away from him and held on, feeling fainter and fainter as the fire licked across their bodies. She buried her flaming head into his flaming chest to muffle her cries, and all went dark.

*****THE END*****

Please enjoy this preview of the third book in the Gatekeeper's Saga, *The Gatekeeper's Daughter*:

Chapter One: From the Ashes

The smell of ash permeated the air, and the cry of birds echoed over the valley. Therese's mouth was dry, her lips parched. She opened her sleepy eyes, her lashes momentarily sticking together, and found her face pressed against Than's chest. The pain had finally stopped. She knew exactly where she was.

She wasn't sure how long she'd been asleep on the altar beside Than beneath the Grecian skies at the base of Mount Kronos outside of Demeter's winter cabin, but her last memory was of the pungent scent of burning flesh, and that had been replaced by the fresh smell of morning dew. Blinking her dry eyes to produce tears, she wondered at the gray papery flakes of ash covering the two of them like dirty snow, which, when she flicked it from her arm, lifted in the air and floated before drifting to the ground. She shuddered, realizing she was brushing away bits of her old self.

Than met her bewildered gaze and gave her a hesitant smile.

"You okay?" he asked.

"We're glowing. Like embers."

"Like gods." He leaned in and kissed her forehead. "My grandmother's method worked. The transformation was a success. You should see how beautiful you look." He propped himself up on his elbows, gazing lazily at her.

"What?"

He pulled a mirror from thin air and handed it to her. She gasped at her own reflection. Her eyes were brighter, her hair shinier, gleaming like the sun. Even her skin and teeth were impeccable, in spite of the flakes of ash peppering her face.

She was also much brighter than humans. Humans. It felt weird not to be included in that category anymore. And she was drop-dead gorgeous. Every one of her features was in better harmony with all the others. She looked airbrushed. Then she had this thought: "I look like my mother." She blinked her eyes several times. Tears formed but didn't fall. She was a goddess.

Her mouth dropped open. "Does this mean...?"

He smiled and nodded, a soft chuckle playing from his throat.

She jumped to her feet and brushed more of the ash from her arms, her legs. What was she wearing? The short white tunic was the only part of her not covered in the gray flakes. When she touched the silk, her dusty hand tainted it.

"I put that on you, just before you woke up," Than explained.

Blood rushed to her cheeks. Did that mean he saw her naked?

The soft chuckle played from his throat once more. "Your modesty is..."

"What?" She hadn't meant that defensive edge in her voice.

"Sweet."

She relaxed a bit and smiled back at him, handing over the mirror, which immediately vanished. "I can't believe this. Am I dreaming?" She pushed off the ground and soared above Than, not quite reaching the treetops surrounding them. Disappointment quaked through her as she landed on her feet in front of the altar. "Are you a figment?"

"You're not dreaming, and I'm not a figment. That little test of yours won't work anymore, now that you can really fly."

"Now that I can...what? Are you saying I can fly?"

"You don't have very high expectations for what it means to be a god."

"I can fly? While I'm awake?" She jumped up into the air, turning somersaults just above Than's head. "I can fly! Woohoo!" Images from *Peter Pan* rushed to her, and, though she laughed at herself, she didn't stop twirling in the air.

Than shook his head. "Come back down here, you crazy girl."

She continued to turn and glide across the sky, daring to go higher, above the trees. "Whoa," she cried when she wobbled and dropped a few feet. Then, confident again, she soared up to the clouds. "Wheeee!!!" Slowly, she descended, feet first, back to the ground, but before she landed, another idea struck her. She took off running up the mountain and was halfway there in seconds. "Look how fast I can run!" Spotting a boulder wedged in the mountainside, she stopped, tugged at it, easily loosening it from the surrounding earth, and lifted it above her head. "Look how strong I am!" Her voice echoed throughout the valley.

"So I can finally kiss you without killing you, and you'd rather fly and lift heavy rocks?"

She giggled and flew to the altar and lay beside him, propping her head on an elbow. "Sorry. I'm all yours." Then, as Than's face moved near hers, she frowned.

"What's wrong?"

"Can we take a shower somewhere? We're both covered in ash." She shuddered again. Yuck. Her own dead body. She'd like to get clean of it as soon as possible.

Than snapped his fingers and a black cloud appeared above them. The cloud opened and dropped cool, refreshing rain.

"Mmm." Therese lifted her face to it and allowed it to cascade down her cheeks, neck, shoulders. "Can I do that, too? Make it rain?"

He swept her wet hair out of her eyes. "Do you really want an education on what it means to be a god? Right now?" With each word, he moved his lips nearer to hers.

"No." She looked at his mouth. "No, not really."

He reached his lips towards her, but she stopped him once again.

"Now what?"

"You burned, too. I saw you pour the kerosene all over yourself. Why?"

He cupped her chin. "I didn't want you to go through that alone."

"Wow. That's so…"

He covered her lips with his as the exhilarating rain softly washed away their ashes and reinvigorated her. She slipped her arms around his neck and pressed her body against his. He pushed her hip down onto the altar and lay half on top of her, crushing her, but she didn't mind, wanting to be as close to him as possible, making every part of her touch every part of him. She curled a leg over his and reveled at the sound of a moan escaping from his lips.

"Oh, Than. I can't believe it. We're finally together."

He snapped his fingers, and the rain stopped, and the morning sunshine warmed and dried them as they kissed, caressed, and stroked one another on Demeter's altar.

Memories of Than anointing her body—every inch of it—with ambrosia, his hands stroking her, quickly but lovingly, filled her with desire.

"Maybe we should go somewhere more private," Than whispered.

Therese nodded, but asked, nearly breathless, "What happened to your mom and grandma?"

Than stopped and sat up. "That's a good question."

Therese sat up, too. "Are you worried?"

"They gave me the vial of ambrosia. They could be in trouble."

"We need to find out."

"I've just disintegrated and dispatched to Mount Olympus to look for them."

"How do you do that?"

"Comes with the job."

"Can I do it?"

"I don't think so, but, ultimately, it'll depend on your purpose."

Just then Therese heard her aunt's voice calling to her, as though she were right there with them. "Oh my god."

"What's wrong?"

"Nothing." She tried to ignore it. "What purpose?"

He leaned back once again on his elbows. "Every god and goddess must serve humankind or the world in some way. We have to find a purpose for you, or this transformation won't last."

Therese hopped from the altar to her feet. "You never mentioned that." It seemed like pretty important information, too. "My god, how much time do I have?"

"I'm not sure, but don't worry."

She frowned, unhappy with his vague answer. She didn't think she had it in her to go through the transformation process again. The anticipation of burning to death had been horrible; the actual pain of burning alive had been worse. "I need a better answer than that. I didn't just burn to death for nothing."

"My grandmother will know. I'm looking for her, so be patient. Hephaestus just told me he hasn't seen her, but that I'm not allowed in the palace. He's going in to ask for me."

Therese heard her aunt again: "Please, Therese, wherever you are. Please come home."

She covered her face with her hands. The voice, full of desperation, seemed so close; her aunt's mouth might have been at her ear.

Than god traveled to her side. "What's wrong?"

"I didn't think about how I would be able to hear my aunt. She's talking to me, begging me to come home. How long have I been gone?"

"A few days."

Therese sat on the ground and covered her face again. "She's in full panic. I knew this would be hard—leaving her and everything—but I didn't know I would hear her crying for me. I can't bear it."

"It's worse than I thought."

Therese lifted her head. "What?"

"My mom and grandmother are being held prisoners at Mount Olympus and are awaiting trial, which we thought could happen, but..." He pulled Therese up to her feet.

"But what?"

"They're coming for us."

"Now? What'll we do?"

He shook his head.

She grabbed his hand and pointed to the top of the mountain. "Let's run and hide. Come on. There could be a cave." What was she thinking? They could go anywhere. "Let's go to China!"

"I'm disintegrated in thousands of places. There's no way I can hide. But you could."

"I'm not leaving you."

Therese wrapped her arms around his waist and pressed her cheek to his chest, the pure joy she felt moments ago vanishing. She hadn't thought completely through the consequences, and they didn't look good. His mother and grandmother were being tried in court. Her aunt and uncle were worried sick, her aunt crying out to her. And now the other gods were coming for them.

Just then roots from the ground at their feet shot up and coiled themselves around Than and Therese's legs, climbing higher and higher, cold and abrasive, ensnaring them in a net of plant. Therese screamed and Than pulled at the roots, to no avail, and soon they were encased in a kind of cocoon. Therese clung to Than, her new heart pounding, her new blood coursing through her limbs. Although she was stronger than she'd ever been in her life, it wasn't enough to break free of the trap. Then she felt the invisible plastic wrap itself around them, recognized the feeling of god travel, and the next instant, she and Than were standing in the middle of the court surrounded by the gods of Mount Olympus.

To order the next book in the saga, please go to: evapohlerbooks.com/books.

For more information about Eva Pohler's Gatekeeper's Saga, please visit http://www.evapohler.com.

33047433R00129

Made in the USA
Middletown, DE
27 June 2016